HE

KT-165-455

Please return on or before the latest date above.
You can renew online at *www.kent.gov.uk/libs*
or by telephone 08458 247 200

CUSTOMER SERVICE EXCELLENCE   **Libraries & Archives**

00884\DTP\RN\07.07   LIB 7

HELL STAGE TO LONE PINE

At Lone Pine Ranch, young Ben Brewer wants to prove himself to the owner, Morgan Hethridge, and his beautiful daughter Josie. But Hethridge's rival is scheming to take over Lone Pine Ranch. To protect the land, Brewer faces the feared gunhawk Calvin Choate. A desperate situation, until old timer Whipcrack Riley steps in. Will his wily ways and his skills driving a stagecoach be enough to help Brewer once the situation gets really rough and the bullets are flying?

JACK DAKOTA

HELL STAGE TO LONE PINE

Complete and Unabridged

LINFORD
Leicester

First published in Great Britain in 2012 by
Robert Hale Limited
London

First Linford Edition
published 2013
by arrangement with
Robert Hale Limited
London

A catalogue record for this book is available
from the British Library.

ISBN 978–1–4448–1633–4

Published by
F. A. Thorpe (Publishing)
Anstey, Leicestershire

Set by Words & Graphics Ltd.
Anstey, Leicestershire
Printed and bound in Great Britain by
T. J. International Ltd., Padstow, Cornwall

This book is printed on acid-free paper

1

It was lucky for the horse that Ben Brewer had been bog riding and had his rope and shovel with him. It was unlucky that he was on his own, making it more difficult to extricate the horse from the quicksand. He jumped from the saddle, quickly fastened one end of his rope round the horse's neck and the other end to the cantle of his saddle. He cinched the saddle as tight as the latigo straps would allow, climbed back into leather and started his horse forward as gently as he could. The strain was immediate and he feared that the rope would draw too tightly round the stranded horse's neck and strangle it. There was a slight movement but not enough.

He dismounted and took off his boots to prevent the mud and sand filling them. Then he took up the short shovel and waded out into the gumbo. He was taking a chance. The mud came over his ankles and he could feel it sucking him down. At least he didn't need to go too far in before he could start digging at the horse's feet, concentrating on the back legs, so that if the animal got any sort of grip with its front legs it wouldn't begin to flounder. The suction gripped like a vice and if the animal had been struggling the situation would have been hopeless. As it was the horse seemed to have passed that stage and succumbed to a dumb hopelessness.

A short period of shovelling was enough to make Brewer's back and shoulders ache and it took all his strength to struggle the few yards back to the edge of the swamp. Once again he mounted the sorrel and touched his spurs to its flanks. The rope took the strain. For a few moments nothing happened, then suddenly something gave way and the sorrel started forward again.

'Come on, boy! You can do it!' Brewer shouted, encouraging the straining animal as the rope took the full weight of the bogged creature.

Brewer looked over his shoulder at the pitiful beast in the swamp. Its head was pulled to one side and there was a wild look in its eye. Brewer was fearful that the effort would be too much for it and its legs would break. Either that or its neck. Slowly they inched forward and then the sorrel came to a stop. For a second time Brewer jumped down and, taking the shovel, began to dig. Then, wearily, he got back into the saddle and urged the sorrel to one more effort. Now the bogged animal began to struggle and Brewer felt encouraged. It had regained its fight and he felt that real progress was being made. If it could just hold out; if its neck and legs could only withstand the strain. He concentrated hard to keep pulling in line with the stranded horse's body. One pull out of line and the further pressure might be the final thing to crick the horse's neck or snap its leg. The sorrel was sweating but it was moving more freely.

Brewer glanced behind one last time. The bogged horse's back legs were coming free and the front ones were loosening. Brewer touched his spurs to the sorrel's flanks, urging it to one last effort. The sorrel strained and then, with a lurch, the stranded horse was loose and struggling up on to firmer ground.

Without losing any time Brewer undid the rope from the cantle and slid to the ground. He drew his knife and cut the rope from the horse's neck. The animal was exhausted, weak and cold. It stood stiff-legged as Brewer threw a blanket over its back and then fed it some oats. He stroked its neck and whispered a few encouraging words into its ear. While he was preoccupied with this he didn't notice a group of three riders bearing down on him until they were almost upon him. Then he became aware of pounding hoofs and looked up. Instinctively he took a step towards the sorrel to reach his Winchester rifle but he was too late. Already the group of riders had drawn to a halt and there was a six-gun in the lead rider's hand, which was pointed at his chest.

'I wouldn't try anythin'.' The man barked.

He was growing to fat and a scar ran down his left cheek. His two companions were nondescript but looked as vicious as a pair of weasels in a sack. Brewer noted the brand marks on their horses: a Buzzard On A Rail. That was Jed Sloane's ranch. Jed Sloane employed some pretty ornery *hombres*, but these were mean even by his standards. In the silence that followed the leader's words Brewer became aware for the first time of the insects which were hovering about his mud-encrusted garments: heelflies. He swatted them away with the back of his hand.

'That hoss,' the man said. 'Looks to me like that's one of ours.'

'See for yourself. It ain't got no markings.'

The man turned to one of his companions. 'What do you reckon, Rafe?' he said. 'Seems to me that hoss is carryin' the Buzzard On A Rail brand.'

'Sure looks that way to me,' the man replied.

'Horse-stealin',' the leader continued. 'That's a mighty serious offence.'

'I ain't stole no horse. That bronc is barely saddle broke. Someone rode it into that swamp and left it there.'

'Ain't no arguin',' the man said. 'You steal someone else's hoss, you got to take what comes.'

'Stealin' hosses is a hangin' offence,' the man referred to as Rafe put in. 'Come on, let's string him up.'

The other one whooped.

'Got us a necktie party!' he shouted. 'What are we waitin' for?'

The leader grinned. 'You see what these boys are like?' he said. 'There just ain't no denyin' 'em when they're lookin' for justice.'

'Shouldn't we let the marshal decide that?' Brewer said.

The three riders guffawed.

'The marshal might hold some sway in Eagle Gulch,' the leader said, 'but out here the Buzzard On A Rail says what's right and what's wrong.'

'This ain't Buzzard On A Rail land.'

The man looked about him. 'Don't see nobody else's cattle,' he said.

'This is free range.'

'Like I say, we ain't here to argue.' He pulled back the hammer of his gun. 'Drop your gun belt and get back on your hoss. We gonna take a ride.'

His two henchmen whooped again. 'Sure are. To the nearest cottonwood tree!'

Brewer paused for just a moment. He had been quickly working out a vague plan which involved putting the rescued horse between him and his attackers, but the horse had walked away and was cropping some grass at a little distance. He looked down the barrel of the six-gun. There was nothing he could do but go along with them. He dropped his guns and climbed into the saddle of the sorrel. One of the Buzzard On A Rail men dropped down and picked up the gunbelt.

'OK. Let's go!' said the leader.

They set off, the Buzzard On A Rail men riding close. Brewer was conscious of the gun aimed at his back. After a short ride they arrived at a stand of trees.

'This will do fine,' the leader said. He turned to one of the others. 'Van, get the rope.'

Brewer was watching for his chance, and as the man dismounted he dug his spurs hard into the flanks of the sorrel. The horse started forward and Brewer flung himself flat along the length of its body. There was a shout behind him and then the crack of a gun. He felt a searing pain in his arm, then the sorrel reared up and sent him crashing to the ground. He scrambled to his feet but in an instant the leader had ridden him down. Brewer looked up to see a horse standing over him and the figure of its rider leaning over with his gun pointed at Brewer's head.

'Get up!' he barked.

Brewer struggled to his feet, clutching his right shoulder. His arm was damaged but there didn't seem to be any broken bones. Before he had time to dwell on his injury he was seized from behind and his arms were pinioned to his sides. Brewer clenched his teeth with the pain. Without any consideration for his wound two of the riders pushed him to his horse. One of them tied a rope around his neck, then they manhandled him up into the saddle. The one called Van gave the other end of the rope to the leader, who dismounted and swung it up and over a low-hanging branch of a tree. The sorrel was restless and was only prevented from moving by one of the riders, who held it by the bridle.

'Say your prayers, Brewer.'

Brewer looked towards the leering face of the leader.

'How come you know my name?' he said.

'I know you like I know your brand. They both stink.'

'And what's yours?'

'What's it to you? You're about to die.'

'A dying man gets to have one last request.'

The man laughed. 'OK. Whatever you want. The name's Choate, Calvin Choate. Remember me in hell.'

'One other thing,' Brewer said.

The rope was already tightening around his neck.

'Yeah. Make it quick.'

'Better take a look behind you.'

The man laughed. 'Nice try,' he said. 'But you'd better come up with something better than that.'

There was a brief pause and then a voice sounded from somewhere in the trees.

'Better do as he says, Choate. Less'n you want to be blown to bits. I got me a shotgun with a hair trigger and it's

10

pointed right between your shoulder blades.'

Brewer watched Choate closely. Choate looked towards his comrades who had half-turned their heads towards the trees. They could see nothing and could give him no kind of sign.

'I don't know what that young man is supposed to have done,' the voice continued, 'but I never held with no kind of lynchin'.' There was another pause and then the voice continued:

'One of you boys better start undoin' that hemp cravat before there's some kind of accident.'

The men's eyes sought those of Choate, who gave an almost imperceptible nod. While one man continued to hold the horse, the other reached up and lifted the rope from Brewer's neck and over his head. While he was doing so, Choate seemed to find his voice.

'This *hombre*'s a horse-thief!' he shouted. 'Just so you realize what you're doin'.'

'Now ain't that a coincidence? I just seen a horse lookin' pretty unhappy

11

with itself down by the swamp. Now if my guess is correct and that there's the horse in question, seems to me it ain't carryin' no brand.'

Brewer dropped down from his horse at the same moment that the bushes behind Choate parted and a man stepped out. Even under the circumstances, Brewer was surprised by his appearance. The newcomer was an oldster and he carried a slight limp.

'I suggest you boys just ride away,' he said.

Brewer's eyes were on Choate. The man was caught in a quandary. Choate looked again at the other two and then the situation was resolved for him. Van had obviously seen the oldster and fancied his chances. In a flash his hand had dropped to his holster; his gun was in his hand and spitting lead in an instant but even so the old man was quicker.

The crash of the oldster's shotgun almost coincided with the report of Van's six-shooter but it was Van who fell to the ground. Rafe's gun was in his hand, but as he fired Brewer kicked out and caught the barrel with his foot. The shot flew high and wide as Brewer flung himself upon his assailant and they went down in a tangle, Brewer's hand gripping the other man's gun hand. There was an explosion of shots behind them as they rolled over on the grass. Rafe was on top of Brewer but Brewer kicked out and the man fell backwards.

Springing instantly to his feet, Brewer kicked out again and the gun went flying from Rafe's hand. Brewer moved to pick it up but Rafe had already reached for his other gun and was about to pull the trigger when a shot rang out and he went staggering back, blood pouring from his chest. He looked up once more and tried to raise his gun hand but then fell to his knees. His baffled eyes looked into Brewer's and then, with the question they were asking unanswered, he sank face forward to the ground. His body twitched and he was still.

Brewer looked behind him. The oldster's shotgun was smoking. Near by Choate lay in a crumpled heap but even as Brewer watched he struggled to his feet. Blood flowing down his arm indicated that the oldster's buckshot had inflicted a minor injury.

'Who are you, old man?' he said.

'Someone to avoid,' the oldster replied. 'Now git on your horse and ride before I change my mind about lettin' you have another chance.'

For a moment Choate hesitated. If he had been contemplating resistance he thought better of it. Instead, he mounted his horse, not without difficulty. He looked down at the old timer and spat on the ground.

'I'll remember you,' he said.

'You better,' the oldster replied.

With a last ugly leer Choate jammed his spurs into the horse's flanks and rode off in the direction of the Buzzard On A Rail. The old man turned to Brewer.

'You OK?' he shouted.

'Yeah, more or less.'

In the heat of battle Brewer had forgotten about his shoulder but now he became aware of an intense pain and he suddenly felt weak. He started to walk towards the oldster but before he had gone a few paces he fell to the ground. The last thing he remembered was the grizzled face of the old man bending over him and then he passed out.

When he awakened it was night and he lay in the warm shelter of a campfire. A blackened tripod hung over the flames and there was bacon sizzling in a pan. His shoulder hurt but it had been bound up and bandaged. His neck was sore where the rope had burned it but otherwise he felt OK. He was alone but after a few minutes he heard footsteps and the oldster emerged from some bushes, carrying a blackened tin kettle which he placed on the tripod. The oldster turned and saw him.

'Ah!' he said. 'You've come round. How are you feelin'?'

Brewer tried to sit up but the pain in his shoulder forced him to lie back again.

'Shoulder hurts like hell,' he said.

'Not surprisin',' the oldster replied. 'Took me a good time to prise that bullet outa you. You lost a lot of blood.'

'You took out the bullet?' Brewer said.

'Done a purty good job of it,' the oldster replied. 'Guess that's what comes of practice.'

'You ain't some kind of a sawbones?'

'Nope, but I've picked up plenty of doctorin' in my time. Mad stone for snakebite, bear oil for rheumatism and a drop of this for most anythin' else.'

He pulled a flask from his pocket and proffered it to Brewer.

'Best forty-rod. Take a sip. If it don't make your eyes bleed it'll cure you.'

Brewer took the flask and swallowed a mouthful. Next moment he was sitting up, gasping for breath and coughing and spluttering as the whiskey burned its way down his throat. His

16

head felt like a volcano.

'Yeah, takes you that way at first,' the oldster said. 'There'll be some black coffee pretty soon and I guess a few strips of bacon might grease your innards.'

By the time he had eaten Brewer had to admit he was feeling a lot better. There was a glow in the pit of his stomach and the world seemed a cosier place. He looked across at the oldster. The man seemed to have developed an almost fatherly aura.

'Say,' Brewer said, 'I ain't thanked you yet for savin' my life.'

'Weren't nothin'. Just lucky I happened to be around.'

'I didn't steal that horse,' Brewer said.

'I know you didn't.'

'How can you be so sure?'

''Cause that horse is mine.'

Brewer looked at him and a smile spread across his features.

'Your horse?' he said.

'Yup. Someone stole him from me.

Plumb got away with a good saddle as well. Musta taken it with them after they rode him into the swamp. Maybe one of the same varmints as tried to lynch you. There's a bunch of 'em been on my tail one way and another for the past few days.'

'They ride for the Buzzard On A Rail ranch,' Brewer said. 'Their horses carried the brand.'

'Yeah. Maybe so. Or maybe they bin the ones doin' the horse thievin'. Either way they ain't gonna be doin' it now.'

The oldster pulled out a pack of Bull Durham. After building himself a smoke he offered the pack to Brewer.

'You punchin' for anybody?' he asked. 'Looked to me you got the equipment.'

'I ride for the Lone Pine.'

'Is that so? What sort of a spread is that?'

'Small but growin'. Mr Hethridge, he's the owner. A real nice man. Gave me my first job as a wrangler.'

'You liked hosses?'

'Sure did.'

'Yeah. Guess you still do, otherwise you wouldn't have put yourself to the bother of rescuin' old Flume.'

'Old Flume?'

'That's what I called him. A throwback to my prospectin' days.'

Brewer's head was pleasantly fuzzy and the oldster's words made little impression.

'Guess you never bin out to the diggin's?' the oldster remarked.

For a while they lay back in silence. The night was still. Brewer reached out for the coffee pot but his hand slipped and he almost fell forward into the flames.

'Here, let me do that,' the oldster said. He poured the coffee into Brewer's tin cup. 'What's your name?' he asked.

'Brewer. Ben Brewer. What's yours?'

'Riley. First name's Rufus but folks call me Whipcrack. That's another throwback, on account of my time stage-drivin' for the Jackass Mail.'

Although Brewer's head was growing more and more hazy he had a vague sense that he was asking a lot of questions.

'Jackass Mail?'

The oldster grinned. 'A bit before your time, young 'un,' he said. 'The San Antonio and San Diego Mail, to give it its proper name. Coach used to be driven by half a dozen mules. San Antonio to Fort Yuma.'

He paused, his cigarette drooping from a corner of his mouth, and looked up at the stars. He seemed to relish the memory. After a few moments of reminiscence he turned back to Brewer.

'You say you ride for the Lone Pine?'

Brewer nodded. 'Mr Hethridge. He's a good man.'

'I'm at a bit of a loose end right now. Could do with takin' stock, as it were. You figure this Mr Hethridge might consider takin' on a new hand? Leastways, for the round-up season.'

'Sure,' Brewer said. 'I could ask about it for you. I work hard and Mr Hethridge likes me. I could certainly ask him for you.'

'Well, that would be real nice,' the oldster said with a smile on his features. 'I reckon Mr Hethridge would listen to a trusted hand like you.'

'He sure would,' Brewer said. 'And it would be real nice to have you along.'

They finished their cigarettes. The fire died down and they drank the last dregs of coffee. The oldster got to his feet and went to check the horses. When he returned he was carrying his shotgun.

'Just in case we have any visitors,' he said.

'What? You reckon we need to keep watch?'

'Nope. Let's just say I'll sleep with one eye open.' He laid the rifle down beside his bedroll. 'Tell you what,' he said, as if he had just been struck by a sudden thought. 'Why don't you have that old horse? I ain't got much use for him these days.'

'Horse?' Brewer repeated. 'What horse?'

The oldster chortled softly. 'Why, Flume, of course.'

'I couldn't take your hoss,' Brewer said.

'I got the burro,' Whipcrack replied. 'Sorry I ain't got the saddle to give you but I reckon you got a few spare back at the ranch. Take him. Put him in with the rest of the remuda if you like.'

'Well, that's real nice of you,' Brewer said. 'Come to think about it, I guess I got a bit of a soft spot now for the old fella considerin' all the trouble he put me through to get him out of that swamp.'

'Good. He's yours. Reckon I'll be turnin' in.'

Brewer lay back. He felt warm and drowsy and when he looked up, the stars seemed to be spinning in the sky. He closed his eyes. Near by, the oldster was soon listening to the sound of his snores.

'Old Forty,' he mused. 'Best medicine in the warbag. Especially laced with morphine. Could be a late start in the mornin'.'

*   *   *

The Lone Pine ranch house occupied a good strategic point at the crest of some gently rising ground backed with trees which allowed its occupants a good view over the lush flatlands towards the Deep Fork River. The river was more of a stream but deep in places. The house itself was built on two floors with timber from the creek. Some shade trees stood nearby together with the tall pine which gave the ranch its name. The rooms were cool and spacious. A raised veranda ran all around. Behind it were several other buildings comprising a chuck-house, a bunk-house, and a barn with a couple of corrals in its rear. The ranch was small but occupied some prime land and Morgan Hethridge grazed upwards of 1,000 head of cattle. On this morning he was taking time out to do some paperwork, sitting in a chair on the veranda, when he heard familiar footsteps and looked up to see his daughter Josie coming round a corner of the house. She had been feeding the hens and was carrying a basket with eggs she had gathered from the coop.

'Look,' she said.

She held the basket out.

'They're doin' well,' Hethridge replied. 'If the cows don't work out, we can always run a poultry farm.'

She laughed, mounted the steps to the porch and proceeded to the kitchen. In a few minutes she came out again.

'Any sign of Brewer?' she asked.

'Not yet.'

'He should have been back yesterday. Haven't any of the men seen him?'

Her father gave her a quizzical glance. 'You seem to be very concerned?' he said.

She tossed her head. 'Just wonderin' what's become of him,' she replied.

She affected to be uninterested but Hethridge noticed the slight flush which spread along her neck and cheeks.

'He'll be by soon,' he said. 'Probably found he had plenty to do and stayed out at one of the line shacks.'

He realized as he spoke the words that he was dissimulating as much as his daughter, but he didn't like to admit his concern. Anyway, Brewer could look after himself. His daughter sat down next to him and as he looked at her he was reminded again of his wife. Although Josie didn't really resemble her, there was something about his daughter that recalled her so intimately. It was something more subtle than looks, something to do with her gestures and mannerisms, something to do with her particular style of femininity. Sometimes when Josie moved or looked at him in a certain way it was almost like having his wife back again, but it was only a momentary sensation. The pain of missing her was something altogether more permanent.

'Like a coffee?' she said.

'Yeah. That would be nice.'

She disappeared into the house again and Hethridge returned to his papers. After a time he looked up and saw two figures approaching. One was Brewer but the other he didn't recognize. Brewer was riding the sorrel and leading another horse while the other man sat astride a burro. As they got closer Hethridge eyed the newcomer more closely. He certainly cut an unexpected sight. He was small and thin and his uncovered head was bald except for some white locks which hung down over the back of his neck. He wore a checked shirt which was open at the front to reveal some further scraps of white hair and he didn't wear boots but what looked like moccasins.

'Now I wonder where Brewer collected that old-timer?' Hethridge muttered.

He had been so concentrated on observing the oldster that he had not taken account of the younger man. Now he noticed the bandaged shoulder and the way the youngster was slumped forward in the saddle. He got to his feet and ran out into the yard to meet them at the same moment as his daughter emerged with the coffee. She set it down on the rail and rushed out to join her father.

'What happened?' Hethridge barked.

For the first time he saw the red welts across Brewer's throat.

'I'm all right,' Brewer replied.

He slid from the saddle, staggering a little as he hit the ground. 'I had a spot of trouble but I was lucky to get some help from this gentleman.'

He turned to the oldster who had dropped from the burro. 'Let me introduce my friend, Mr Whipcrack Riley.'

The oldster gave a faint nod and held out his hand for Hethridge to shake.

'Glad to meet you,' Hethridge said. 'Any friend of Ben is a friend of mine.'

He turned to Josie who was standing behind him looking anxiously at Brewer. 'Why don't you pour some of that coffee?' he said.

She looked from one to the other of the men standing in the yard and Hethridge could see there were tears in her eyes. He glanced at Brewer but the youngster was facing Riley and it didn't appear that he had noticed them. Josie turned on her heels and ran back up the stairs and into the house.

'Jarrett!' Hethridge called.

After a moment a man came running from the bunkhouse.

'Take charge of the hosses and the mule,' Hethridge said. 'Gentlemen, in addition to that coffee, I think we could all do with somethin' a little stronger.'

He led the way up the steps and into the ranch house. Indicating to the two men that they should take a seat, he went to a cabinet and poured three stiff drinks from a decanter of brandy.

'OK,' he said. 'I reckon you'd better tell me the whole story.'

By the time Brewer had finished Hethridge was fuming.

'That dang-blasted coyote Sloane!' he exclaimed. 'He's been causin' trouble for a long time but I never figured he'd go this far!'

'It weren't him,' Brewer said. 'Maybe some of his boys just got a little out of hand.'

'It's all part of his programme of harassin' the Lone Pine till we get tired and sell. He's been eyein' this place ever since I took it on. And it ain't as if he hasn't got enough land already. He's by far the biggest rancher in the territory. Maybe it's just greed on his part, but I sometimes have a feelin' there's more to it than that.'

'Well, maybe we'd better just let this one pass,' Brewer said. 'After all, no harm's been done at the end of the day and thanks to Mr Riley those varmints sure paid for it.'

Hethridge turned to the old timer. 'Sure am grateful,' he said. 'Brewer ain't just one of the ranch hands. He's been like a son to me, the son I never had, ever since he first came here as a boy. Seems like we got you to thank for rescuin' him and if there's anythin' I can do to let me show my appreciation, you only have to say what it is.'

'That's mighty nice of you,' the oldster said, 'but I was just doin' what any decent *hombre* would have done.'

There was a pause while the three of them finished their brandies. There was no sign of the coffee, Josie had taken to her bedroom where she lay on her bed resting her tear-stained face on the pillow.

'As a matter of fact,' Brewer said, 'there is somethin' you can do. Mr Riley is lookin' for a job just at the moment. I said you might consider takin' him on as a hand, at least till the round-up's finished.'

Hethridge jumped to his feet. 'Of course,' he said. 'Consider it done.'

'If'n you're sure,' Riley said.

'Sure? 'Course I'm sure. After what you did, you're welcome to stay here at the Lone Pine for as long as you like. Even apart from that, I could do with a bit of extra help.' He turned to Brewer. 'Why don't you take Mr Riley to the bunkhouse? Let him get settled in and then show him about the place.'

The oldster got to his feet. 'Ain't gonna take me no time to do that,' he said. 'Just so long as ol' Sally is taken care of.'

'Ol' Sally?'

'The mule,' Riley said. 'Me an' her's bin together a long whiles now. A hoss is fine but give me a burro any day. She's tougher and can carry a lot more load.'

He turned to Brewer. 'You're doin' me a favour takin' that packhorse off my hands.'

As they were talking, Brewer had been looking for Josie to reappear but there was no further sign of her or the coffee. If he had known that she had gone to her room where she lay on the bed, her tear-stained face buried in a pillow on his account, he would not have believed it. As far as he was aware, the best he could hope for was to worship her from afar and look forward to every moment when he might just get a glimpse of her. She was the rancher's daughter. Morgan Hethridge might have taken him in and more or less adopted him, but to imagine that his daughter might be attainable was going just a little too far.

2

Next morning Hethridge was just finishing his breakfast when he heard the sound of approaching hoofs. Getting to his feet, he peered out of the window to see Marshal Zwing Burke dismounting in the yard and tying his horse at the hitchrack.

'Now why would the marshal be ridin' out this way?' he muttered to himself.

He had only met the marshal on a small number of occasions when he had business in town, but there was something about Burke that he wasn't sure about. Maybe it was just that he was young and untried. Hethridge didn't entirely trust his judgement. Maybe it was a mere physical reaction against his greasy slicked-back hair and duds that were just a little too fancy for a working lawman. Even from a distance he couldn't help noticing the marshal's ivory-handled guns. He dropped the curtain, moved to the door and stepped on to the veranda.

'Mornin', Marshal,' he said. 'Hope you weren't expectin' breakfast 'cause I just finished it.'

'It ain't breakfast I'm after,' the marshal replied.

Burke looked behind him. A couple of the Lone Pine cowboys had come from the bunkhouse and were standing near by.

'Well, what is it then?' Hethridge said.

The marshal turned back. He looked slightly uncomfortable. He dug into an inside pocket and produced a piece of folded paper.

'I got a warrant here,' he said, 'for the arrest of Ben Brewer. I also got one for the arrest of another man, an unknown. I've reason to believe he might be somewhere on your property.'

Hethridge advanced a couple of paces.

'Let me take a look at that document,' he said.

The marshal handed it over and Hethridge unfolded it. For a few moments his eyes scanned the paper and then he handed it back to the marshal.

'I don't know too much about the law,' he said, 'but that thing don't seem to be rightly drawn up to me.'

'It's legal,' the marshal replied.

'What's Brewer supposed to have done?'

'He's wanted for horse-thievin' and murder.'

'In that order?'

The marshal shifted uneasily. 'Why don't you just hand him over?' he said. 'I don't aim to stand here arguin' over the matter.'

Hethridge ran his fingers across his chin before looking over the marshal's head.

'Any of you boys seen Brewer?' he shouted to the men standing in the yard.

'Brewer? Nope, ain't seen him since day before yesterday.'

'How 'bout you, Aldridge?'

'Nope. Can't say as I've seen him recently either.'

Hethridge turned to the marshal. 'There you are,' he said. 'I'd like to oblige but nobody's seen Brewer around. Last time I saw him he was headed for the brakes to do some brush poppin'. That was yesterday. Come to think of it, I wonder what could have happened to him? I'd have expected him back before now.'

'Mind if I take a look around?' the marshal said.

Hethridge laughed. 'Matter of fact, yes I do. Like I just said, Brewer ain't here. Now I suggest you get back on your horse and go back to town.'

The marshal hesitated before turning and untying his horse.

'You could be running the risk of getting on the wrong side of the law yourself,' he said. 'Harbouring a wanted criminal is a serious crime.'

'If I see Brewer, I'll let you know,' Hethridge replied.

'Like I said, there's someone else we're lookin' for. Don't know his name or anythin' about him but he's an oldster; carries a shotgun. Don't suppose you've seen anythin' of him either?'

'Why would that be likely?'

The marshal spat. 'Don't think this is the end of the matter,' he said. 'I'll be back, if necessary with a posse. I'd advise you not to let it get to that stage.'

'Thanks for the advice,' Hethridge replied. 'Nice to know you're on the job. Makes us ordinary folk feel kinda safe.'

Burke climbed into the saddle. Wheeling away, he rode out of the yard, almost knocking over one of the ranch hands. Hethridge watched him till he was a long way off, then called to one of the men who were making their way towards the corrals.

'Guthrie, tell Brewer to get over here,' he shouted. 'I need to have a word.'

Guthrie went to the bunkhouse but

Brewer wasn't there. He had gone round to the corrals and was leaning against a corral pole watching the horse Riley had given him. Now that it had been cleaned up and attended to, he could appreciate its lines. It was a piebald pinto stallion, large for its type and well muscled. It was looking at Brewer with a flashing blue eye and its ears were cocked. Brewer could see that it was nervous. Brewer had taken the sling from his arm and shoulder but the wound was painful. Part of him recognized that the wise thing to do would be to give the wound time to heal but he wanted to ride that horse. Hefting the saddle he had brought from the barn, he opened the gate and walked into the corral. The pinto whinnied as he approached and began to back off.

'Steady, old fella,' Brewer said.

Talking softly, he stopped and waited for a few moments before stepping forward again, coming at the horse from an angle. When he was level with the pinto he got a lump of sugar out of his shirt pocket and put it on the palm of his hand. The horse bared its teeth and took it while Brewer stroked it gently on the forehead. Then he moved round, slung the saddle over its back and commenced to tie the cinches. He slipped on the hackamore. The pinto shuffled forward but quieted after a few more words from Brewer. Then Brewer took hold of the saddle horn and went up into the saddle. The horse remained still but its ears were twitching.

Brewer's feet found the stirrups and with his good arm he took hold of the hackamore rope. The pinto tensed. Brewer wasn't sure what to expect. If the horse decided to buck and rear, he would hang on for as long as he could. In deciding that, he had forgotten all about his injury. The pinto began to move its neck but its head was held high. That was a good sign that it wouldn't do a lot of bucking. *Maybe I should have had a few words with Riley*, Brewer reflected. He had no real idea how saddle-broke the animal was, he had only instinct and observation to go by. That and the experience he had gained during his days as a wrangler. The pinto had accepted the saddle OK but maybe that just signalled the fact that it was a bronco.

While the horse remained still he continued talking to it before gently touching his spurs to the animal's flanks. The horse tossed its head and moved off sideways, but a firm pull on the hackamore rope brought it straight again. It shook its head from side to side and then began to weave, zigzagging its way across the empty corral. Brewer let it have its way until its head went down and he realized that it was trying to get its head between its forelegs, which might herald a jump. He hauled firmly on the rope. The horse tossed its head again, then it settled to a steady walk and Brewer knew that he had nothing to fear. The horse had registered mild dissent but that was all it was.

Leaning forward, he ran his hand down the pinto's mane, still talking gently. Then he brought the pinto to a halt and slid from the saddle. He reached again into his pocket and brought out another lump of sugar. Only then did he remember his damaged arm and realize that he had a spectator. Sitting on the top rail of the corral was Whipcrack Riley.

'How long you been there?' Brewer said.

'Couple of minutes. Long enough to see you make friends with that there hoss.'

'He's already broke but he's still got plenty of spirit. A horse is no good without spirit.'

'Yeah,' the oldster said.

He dropped down from the rail and stood for a few moments. Brewer was expecting him to add something but before he could do so they were interrupted by a voice calling out to Brewer. It was Guthrie, who had just found him.

'Brewer, the boss wants to see you.'

'What, right now?'

'Yup. He wants you to go round to the ranch house.'

Brewer looked at Riley.

'Did he say what he wanted?'

'Nope, but the marshal's just paid a courtesy call.'

'Go on,' Riley said. 'I'll see to the hoss.'

Brewer followed Guthrie, who went into the bunkhouse. Brewer mounted the steps to the veranda and paused at the ranch house door. Miss Josie might be inside and he needed to compose himself for a moment. Then he knocked on the door.

'Come in!' Hethridge's voice called.

Brewer entered, taking a quick look about him as he did so. There was no sign of Josie but her father was standing by the far wall where a rack of guns stood above the fireplace. He was still reaching up and it looked like he had just replaced one.

'I understand you want to see me,' Brewer began.

Hethridge waved him to a chair. 'I

just had a visit from the marshal,' he said. 'He came to get you.'

'What do you mean? I don't understand.'

'He claimed he had a warrant for your arrest.'

'Arrest!' Brewer exclaimed. 'On what charge?'

'Horse theft and murder is what he said.'

'Is this somethin' to do with what happened day before yesterday?'

'Yes.'

'But it ain't me he should be arrestin'! It should be that ornery galoot Choate he's after.'

Hethridge's face was grim. 'Of course you're right, but that don't mean a damn thing. I never took to Marshal Burke and now it looks like he's under Sloane's influence. I won't put it any stronger than that. Seems like Sloane has got to the marshal on Choate's behalf.'

Brewer got to his feet. 'I'll ride to Eagle Creek and have a word with the marshal. See if I can straighten things out. He must have got the wrong end of the stick.'

'No you won't,' Hethridge replied. 'Somehow, I don't think that would be a very good idea. Not unless you want to end up in jail, or somethin' worse.'

'But surely he'll understand when I explain what happened.'

'It ain't a question of whether he understands or not. Especially if I'm right about him and Sloane bein' in cahoots over this.'

'Then what do you suggest?'

'Burke reckons he's comin' back this way with a posse in tow. Seems to me the best thing you can do is make yourself scarce for a while. There's an old line shack nobody's used for a long time at the far end of the west range. Nobody knows about it and nobody goes out that way because it's right on the edge of the badlands. Curly Evans knows the way there. I'll get him to show you.'

'I think I know the place. But how

long do you intend I should stay there?'

'Until this blows over.'

'I don't know. I still think — '

Before he could complete the sentence Hethridge interrupted with a shout: 'You'll do what I say!'

In the silence which followed his outburst they both looked at each other in surprise.

'I'm sorry,' Hethridge said. 'I didn't mean to shout like that.'

'Sure. It's OK.'

'Let me handle the marshal. I'll let you know just as soon as it's safe for you to come back. It's not as if you'll be far away and if necessary we can keep in touch through Curly. Go and get saddled up.'

Brewer moved to the door.

'I've just had another thought,' Hethridge said. 'The marshal mentioned somethin' about Whipcrack Riley. Maybe you'd better take him along with you.'

Brewer paused. 'Seems like him and me are bein' thrown together some,' he said.

'From what you've told me,' Heth-ridge replied, 'you could have a worse partner to stand alongside when trouble's stirrin'.'

As he made his way to the bunk-house, Brewer looked up at the windows on the second floor and was taken aback to see Josie looking down at him. He was suddenly confused and could think of nothing better to do than give a tepid smile. Then, realizing that she probably couldn't make out his expression, he made to wave his hand. It was an awkward gesture. Josie's figure disappeared and he continued on his way, feeling at once both disturbed and foolish.

Shortly afterwards Brewer and Riley rode out of the yard accompanied by Curly Evans. Brewer had decided to take the pinto and Riley had opted for a buckskin, leaving his burro behind. As they left, Brewer looked in vain for a last glimpse of Josie.

'I ain't altogether happy about this,' Riley remarked.

Brewer turned his attention to the oldster. 'Happy? Happy about what?'

'About cuttin' and runnin'.'

Brewer thought about it for a moment.

'Nope,' he replied. 'Neither am I.'

They rode on in silence, each lost in his own thoughts. Brewer was familiar with this part of the range but Whipcrack took time to observe things around him. The range was greening up and groups of cattle dotted the landscape. Some of the ranch hands could be seen hunting out cattle and occasional clouds of dust indicated where stock was being bunched and moved. For a time they rode parallel to the creek, then Curly turned his horse towards the water and they splashed through at a ford where the river ran wide and shallow. They continued riding up the further slope and gradually the nature of the country began to change. The good grass gave way to thinner, scanter pasture and they entered a region of broken country with patches of mesquite thicket and prickly pear.

'Not been out this way much myself,' Brewer remarked. 'We're pretty well out of Lone Pine limits.'

Curly had overheard. 'There'll be cattle in the draws,' he said. 'It's goin' to be a tough old job roustin' them out. Could take days. That's why they built the old cabin out here in the first place.'

They rode a little further, then Curly pointed ahead.

'There it is,' he said.

Brewer strained his eyes but could see nothing.

'There, beside the trees.'

'I see it,' Riley replied.

Up ahead of them was a spot where a narrow trickle of water came down through the brush, creating a little space where a few old cottonwood trees stood amidst the undergrowth. In one corner stood the line cabin and in its immediate rear a barnlike structure provided shelter for a couple of horses. A pole corral stood empty and forlorn.

'Ain't much but she'll do,' Riley said.

They dropped from their saddles and approached the cabin. Curly put his shoulder to the door and it opened at his push. There was only the one room, containing a couple of bunks, a cheap pine table and two straight-backed chairs. A wooden box on the far wall held various items of food and some utensils like tin plates, knives and spoons and there was a small wood-burning stove.

'Food's still OK,' Curly said. 'You'll find some logs outside. Chopped 'em myself.'

'You were up here recently?' Brewer asked him.

'Yup. Couple of weeks ago, pushin' strays back. Spent one night here.'

Riley's eyes swept the room. 'Like I say, she ain't too bad as far as hoodens go,' he said. Curly moved towards the door. 'Make yourselves at home,' he quipped. 'I'll be back just as soon as Mr Hethridge gives me the word it's OK for you to return.'

Brewer and Riley accompanied him outside and watched as he stepped into leather and rode away.

'I still ain't happy about it,' Riley said. He looked at the pile of logs stacked outside the cabin. 'That Curly didn't chop no logs,' he said. 'Can you see any tree that's been felled?'

'You got a point,' Brewer said. 'Guess they musta been here for a while. Hell, I don't care. Let's just take an armful and get that stove goin'. It's gettin' mighty chilly.'

They carried some of the logs in and, while Brewer got the stove going, Riley saw to the feeding and stabling of the horses. Then they set about preparing a meal. By the time they had finished the place seemed a lot more comfortable. They built themselves smokes and lay on the bunks.

'Shoulda bought some cards or checkers,' Brewer said.

'I don't play,' Riley replied.

'My shoulder still hurts,' Brewer said. 'Maybe a few days out here ain't no bad thing,' Riley answered. 'Give the wound a chance to heal.'

'My neck don't feel so good neither.' Brewer inhaled and coughed.

'I reckon there must be cattle in some of those draws that have probably been in there for years,' Riley said. 'What do you say we haze some of 'em out while we're here? There's room in that old corral.'

Brewer laughed.

'You're figurin' same as me,' he said. 'We're gettin' stir crazy already.'

'Take your mind off those injuries,' Riley replied.

The cabin was warm and Brewer got up and opened the door. Outside the night was oddly luminous. A moon sailed high and a breeze had sprung up, rustling through the cottonwoods.

'Sure is a lonesome spot,' Brewer said.

Riley joined him in the open. Suddenly the darkness was rent by a flash and the crack of a rifle shot. Both men dropped down and then slipped back through the open door.

'Guess we got kinda careless,' Riley snapped. 'Musta made a pretty good target outlined against the lamplight.'

He leaned across the table and blew out the lamp, then took his shotgun, which was leaning against a wall. Brewer reached for his Winchester.

'How did they know we were here?' Brewer said.

'If it's Choate with maybe some of his friends from the Buzzard On A Rail, they must have Hethridge's spread under surveillance.'

'Unless it's somebody else?'

'That don't seem very likely.'

'Then it didn't make much difference us comin' here.'

'Coulda made things worse. But somebody just made a mistake letting us know they're out there. Guess he couldn't resist when he saw a chance to pick us off. Lucky he wasn't a better shot. But they've got us isolated. Could be a rough night.'

There was a window in the cabin, an

empty space with shutters but no glass. They took up positions on either side. Riley held up his finger to indicate silence and they listened intently for any sounds of movement outside. They could hear nothing but the snicker of the horses. Brewer looked up at the oldster.

'Maybe we should make a break for it,' he said. 'It's dark without the lamp. If we move fast we should be able to make it to the horses.'

Riley was silent, weighing up the options: whether to stay and make a fight for it or follow Brewer's suggestion. It would help if they knew how many gunmen were out there. His instincts told him there were a good number of them. Choate was out for revenge. But there seemed to be more to this. He recalled what Hethridge had had to say about Jed Sloane. Whatever Choate's personal motives might be, it tied in with the pressure Sloane seemed to be applying to gain control of the Lone Pine. Well, first things first.

'You could make a run for it while I keep you covered.'

Any further speculation was suddenly cut short as a fusillade of shooting broke out. Bullets thudded into the wood of the cabin and one shot smashed through the shutter just above Brewer's head, narrowly missing him before ricocheting off one of the tin utensils on the shelf. Brewer and Riley began firing through the partly opened shutters but they were driven back by the sheer fury of the cannonade from outside. Shots were coming in through the window gaps and the walls of the shack shook with the force of the bullets raining down on them.

'Stay low!' Riley shouted.

They flung themselves on the hard-packed dirt floor. Slugs were coming through the walls and the racket outside was deafening.

'We gotta to do something!' Brewer called.

Riley looked about him. Standing on the table was the kerosene lamp, and there was another hanging on a bracket.

'OK!' he yelled back. 'Here's what we do. We light those lamps and throw 'em out of the window. They'll explode and start a fire. That might just distract those varmints long enough for us to make a break.'

'Yeah. Let's give it a try.'

Brewer kneeled up and got the lamp from the table while Riley crawled to the wall on which the bracket hung. Quickly he got to his feet and removed it. In another minute they had lit the lamps.

'OK!' Riley shouted. 'We'll throw 'em together towards the front of the cabin. As soon as we have, start runnin'.'

'Sure your knees will carry you?' Brewer grinned.

'Yeah, but I ain't so sure about the hips!'

They looked at one another, then, reaching up, they hurled the kerosene lamps through the window. Then they moved swiftly to the door. Outside there was an explosion, instantly followed by another.

Then they were on their feet and running through the door, bent low and keeping to the wall. There was an instant's pause before shooting recommenced and bullets crashed through the walls of the cabin, tearing up the earth, but it was long enough for them to reach the corner of the building.

It was only a short distance to the barn, but they had no idea of what sort of coverage their attackers had of the rear of the building. Even as he hurtled forward, it occurred to Brewer that they might already have taken possession of it, in which case he and Riley were in serious difficulties. A few shots whistled over their heads but it seemed the Buzzard On A Rail boys had mustered most of their forces for the attack at the front and they reached the door of the barn unscathed.

Brewer, getting there first, paused momentarily, then slipped through the doorway, his rifle at the ready. There was no shooting and as his eyes quickly adjusted to the dark he could see that there was nobody there. The two horses were neighing and stamping their feet. Riley followed Brewer into the barn and quickly they started to saddle up the horses while trying to quieten them at the same time. Riley had been worrying about their chances of riding out under the hail of fire that was sure to pursue them but now he saw that the back wall of the barn had fallen in, giving them another way out. With a final tightening of the cinches, he led the way, leading the horse out through the gap. To what extent the surrounding gunmen were aware of what they were doing, he did not know, but as they stepped into leather and touched their spurs to the horses' flanks, there was little in the way of firing, although the rattle and crash of gunshots continued from the front of the building. They were moving quickly now and seemed to have made good their escape when suddenly a bunch of shadowy figures appeared in front of them.

'Keep ridin',' Riley yelled.

Stabs of flame lit the darkness and Riley felt a bullet sing by his cheek, but he kept right on going. One of the men screamed as Riley's horse crashed into him. The others jumped to one side and Riley let blast with his shotgun, catching one of them and sending him spinning to the ground. Then they were through the human barrier.

They heard shouts behind them and a burst of shooting but the bullets went flying harmlessly into the night. Letting the horses have their heads, they galloped on until eventually, feeling that they had put sufficient distance between themselves and the cabin, they slowed the horses to a canter and then to a walk. Drawing rein at last, they scanned their back trail. There was no sign of pursuit. They listened closely but the night was silent.

'That was too close for comfort,' Brewer remarked. He leaned forward and ran his hand over the pinto's mane. 'She's a good horse,' he said.

'Sure. I guess she's taken to you.'

They remained silent for a few moments. The sky was clear and they could see a good distance by the light of the moon and stars. Clumps of mesquite and juniper were patches of darkness on the landscape.

'What do we do now?' Brewer asked.

'Whatever we do, one thing's for sure. Choate ain't gonna give up. Whatever the situation between Hethridge and Sloane, Choate is takin' it personal.'

'And don't forget, we got the marshal lookin' for us too. Might be an idea to make ourselves scarce for a while.'

'Yeah.'

They looked at one another.

'It makes sense,' Brewer said.

There was another period of silence.

'Hell,' Brewer said, 'what's sense got to do with it?'

'Those polecats are probably makin' themselves comfortable right now,' Riley said, 'in our cabin with our gear.'

'I don't reckon they can be allowed to get away with that,' Brewer said.

They continued sitting their horses

while they jammed shells into their guns.

'OK,' Riley said. 'Let's get goin'.'

They wheeled their horses and began to ride back towards the cabin. They travelled at a steady pace this time, their eyes continuing to scan the scene for any signs of pursuit. Presently they came in sight of the cabin. There were horses in the corral and light poured from the windows and the partly opened door. They could hear the sound of voices making merry from inside.

'Eight horses,' Riley said. 'There'll probably be others in the barn.'

'Maybe some still tethered someplace else.'

'They won't be expectin' us,' Riley said. 'I reckon that makes the odds about even.'

Brewer grinned. He drew his Winchester out of its scabbard and Riley hefted the shotgun.

'Ready?'

'Ready!

Applying their spurs, they broke into a gallop. The ground flew beneath the horses' hoofs and as they approached the cabin, at a signal from Riley, they both opened fire. Shots thudded into the walls but a good number rained through the opened doorway and window gaps. Riley began to whoop and Brewer did likewise. A figure appeared in the doorway and went tumbling backwards as a shot took him in the chest. Another figure emerged and Riley's shotgun sent him reeling. The roles were reversed and the Buzzard On A Rail men, taken completely by surprise, were acting in a confused and inappropriate manner.

As Riley and Brewer rode through the yard a couple of men, drawn by the sound of firing, came out of the barn to be felled by a blast of Riley's nine balls to the cartridge buckshot. Drawing his horse to a halt by the corral, Brewer reached down and undid the latch to the gate. It swung open and the frightened horses stampeded through, knocking into each other in their desperation to get away from the pandemonium.

More men had run out into the yard

and were now sent scattering by the pounding hoofs of their own terrified mounts. One man was too slow and with an agonizing scream he went down under the flying hoofs of one of the horses. Brewer and Riley turned and rode back, firing as they went. From somewhere beyond the cabin more figures began to appear, running towards the scene.

'OK!' Riley shouted. 'That should do it for now.'

He whooped again, then the two of them were riding pell-mell away from the scene of confusion. They carried on riding but stopped before they had gone very far.

'No need to worry about pursuit now.' Riley grinned. 'It's gonna take them a hell of a time to find those broncs. If they ever do catch up with 'em.'

Brewer, excited and exhilarated by the action, laughed loudly.

'Wanna go back?' he said.

'It's temptin',' Riley replied, 'but they'll be ready for us this time. Nope, I guess we've given Choate a bit of a lesson. Right now I figure I could do with findin' somewhere to rest up for the night.'

'A bit too much excitement for an oldster?' Brewer quipped.

It was Riley's turn to laugh. 'Yeah,' he replied. 'Guess I'll be needin' my milk.'

He produced a flask from his saddle-bags, opened it and took a long swig. 'Here, have some.'

Brewer took the flask and swallowed the whiskey. 'Hell,' he said as it burnt its way down his throat, 'I should have learned my lesson last time.'

They rode on until eventually they found a suitable place to make camp in the shelter of some bushes. They built a fire and after eating some slabs of bacon with hot coffee, taken from their saddlebags, Riley brought out his pouch of Bull Durham and they both built smokes. They sat back and relaxed till Riley broke the silence.

'What's the story with Jed Sloane and the Buzzard On A Rail?' he said.

'How do you mean?'

'Well, there's obviously things I don't understand. There's more to this business with Choate than meets the eye. Else why would he and the rest of those varmints want to hang you in the first place? They knew that hoss didn't belong to them. And why would the marshal have accepted Sloane's version of events without askin' any questions? There's obviously bad blood between the Buzzard On A Rail and the Lone Pine.'

Brewer inhaled and looked up at the stars.

'You're right,' he said. 'Trouble is, I'm pretty well as much in the dark as you. Since I bin workin' for Mr Hethridge there's always been some ill feelin' between him and Mr Sloane, but just recently it's got a lot worse.'

'In what way?'

'Well, there's been boundary incidents. Mr Hethridge is pretty sure Sloane's been runnin' off some of his cattle. There's been trouble between

Buzzard On A Rail and Lone Pine hands when they've met up in town. When there's any kind of an incident, the marshal seems to take the Buzzard side. Some of our boys have ended up in jail and it just weren't their fault.'

'So what's the problem?'

Brewer shook his head. 'Who knows?' he said. 'But I tell you what. If things carry on this way there's goin' to be a real range war.'

'And if that happens, I guess it would be Sloane who comes out on top.'

Brewer shrugged. 'Not if I can help it,' he said. 'The Buzzard On A Rail is a whole lot bigger but we can put up a good fight if it comes to it.'

'Seems to me that that's just what Sloane wants. He's goading you and if you resist you'll be playin' right into his hands. 'Specially if he's got the marshal on his side and more so if he's employin' gunnies like Choate.'

Silence descended once again. Then Riley spoke once more.

'Ever hear tell of the Plains and

Western Railroad Company?'

'Nope.'

'Not many people have. I picked up some information about them when I was drivin' the Eagle Creek stage, workin' for a man called Jim Drewitt. You know the Eagle Creek stage line, I take it?'

'Sure. Never rode with them though.'

'Well, the Plains and Western is a new company. Seems like there's talk of them building a railroad line out to Eagle Creek. That would mean them buyin' out the Eagle Creek stage line. It would also have other repercussions.'

'Yeah? What?'

'To get to Eagle Creek they'd need to lay a line right across a section of Lone Pine range. That would mean they'd need to pay a lot of money in compensation. Or maybe even buy out the Lone Pine.'

'Mr Hethridge would never think of sellin' up. Now you mention it, I think he's under pressure to do just that and I reckon there's a lot hangin' on the cattle drive, but the Lone Pine means everythin' to him.'

'Well, that's as maybe. But Jed Sloane certainly would sell up.'

'Well, it ain't up to Jed Sloane.'

Riley gave Brewer an exasperated look. Brewer took a moment to think.

'Hell,' he said, 'I see what you mean.'

'Yeah. There's a lot of money at stake. If Jed Sloane could get his hands on the Lone Pine, he'd be in with a chance of makin' a real killin' if those plans to build the railroad go ahead.'

They stopped talking. From somewhere a night bird called and the wind suddenly gusted through the camp as a cloud hid the face of the moon. They smoked another cigarette and then Riley spoke again.

'You get some sleep,' he said. 'I'll stay on guard. Don't reckon there'll be any interruptions but you never know.'

'OK. Wake me when it's my turn.'

Brewer stretched out. Riley took out his six-gun and lay it on the ground beside him.

'Choate is sure gonna feel sore as hell

when mornin' comes,' Brewer said.

Riley grinned. 'Sure is. But by the time he gets round to do anythin' about it, we'll be long gone.'

Brewer lay still for a while, then sat up. Riley was sitting by the dwindling fire and seemed not to have moved.

'Long gone where?' Brewer asked.

The oldster looked over at him and chortled. Brewer gave him a blank look.

'Like I say, where do we go?'

'I guess I'm thinkin' what you're thinkin'.'

'What? Head on back to the ranch?'

Again the oldster chuckled. 'You read my mind.'

'I never did like runnin',' Brewer said.

'We ain't doin' much good out thisaway. I guess Hethridge had our best interests at heart, but I've a feelin' he might just need our help. And I don't like runnin' no more than you.'

He took a long look at Brewer in the flickering light of the fire. 'Maybe you got another reason for gettin' back?' he said.

Brewer looked puzzled.

'I mean Miss Josie.'

'Miss Josie? I don't know what you mean. I never . . . ' He stopped when he saw the knowing look on Riley's face. 'How did you guess? Is it that obvious?'

'Ain't nothin' wrong with bein' a bit sweet on a young lady,' Riley said.

'Yeah. Trouble is, she hardly knows I even exist.'

'Haven't you known each other for quite some time?'

'That's just the problem,' Brewer replied. 'She's so used to me bein' around that she don't notice me any more than one of the hosses.'

'Well, I wouldn't be so sure of that. In fact, I wouldn't be at all surprised if she was thinkin' of you right now.'

Brewer grunted. 'She's the boss's daughter. She ain't gonna give no consideration to a no-hope cow puncher.'

'You're more than that. You said yourself that Hethridge has been lookin' out for you.'

'That's different.'

There was a pause.

'I saw you take on that hoss I give you. Wasn't as hard as you imagined, was it? A lady ain't no hoss but unless you drop your loop there ain't no chance of gettin' her gentled down in the home corral.'

There was no reply. Brewer was thinking about what Riley had said. He had never considered that he might have a chance with Josie. Could there really be a possibility that Riley was right and she could be thinking of him even as he was thinking of her? The thought was oddly disturbing. He lay back and looked up at the sky. Maybe Josie was doing the same. The idea seemed to somehow bind them together. Meanwhile Riley sat on his haunches and dropped another stick on the fire. It blazed up and he resumed his watch.

3

In the dining room of the Palace hotel a meeting was taking place between Jed Sloane, owner of the Buzzard On A Rail ranch, and the director of the Plains & Western Railroad Company, a large florid individual by name of Jackson Cook.

'I wouldn't say anythin' about your plans for the route of the proposed line,' Sloane was saying. 'Leastways, not just for the moment.'

'I think we have an understanding,' Cook replied.

'Like I say, leave it to me to put pressure on the Lone Pine. Give me a couple of weeks and I'll have Hethridge just beggin' to sell the place at any price I care to offer. That way you get the right of way dirt cheap.'

'I could always negotiate directly with Mr Hethridge,' Cook replied.

'There's no way he would sell. Not for choice.'

'Not even for the substantial sums of money the Plains and Western might offer?'

'Nope. It's gonna take a different kind of persuasion.'

'Well, I trust that you are right. At least I'm prepared to give your suggestion a chance. If your . . . ' he paused for a moment, then went on, 'alternative methods fail to produce a result then I may need to rethink the whole situation. Of course the Plains and Western must totally dissociate itself from any action the Buzzard On A Rail may deem necessary.'

Cook rose slowly to his feet. 'A pleasure to do business with you,' he said.

Straightening his frock-coat and taking his hat in his hand, he left the dining room. Soon afterwards the marshal appeared in the doorway and made his way to Sloane's table. Sloane looked at him with an element of distaste.

'Well,' he said. 'Any further news about Brewer?'

'Seems like he took off with the oldster not long after I left the Lone Pine. Choate's on his trail, but to be honest I'm not sure about Choate. Why do you employ him?'

'Choate is an idiot,' Sloane replied. 'But he has his uses. On the evidence so far, I figure I'd have done better to employ a regular polecat.'

'I could get some wanted dodgers out on Brewer and the oldster. Always assumin' you've given me the facts in the case.'

Sloane gave the marshal a hard look. 'Yeah, you do that,' he said.

The marshal got to his feet. 'I'll be in touch.'

Sloane watched him as he walked through the door. Burke was proving to be less malleable than he had expected. As he sat alone at the table a plan was forming in his brain. Choate was a liability, but he was sweet about Hethridge's daughter, Josie. Maybe that was something he could work on. It would involve getting into different territory altogether, but things were speeding up. Cook was applying pressure. There was no avoiding the issue. Something more drastic was required.

When he left the hotel he bent his steps in the direction of the office of Everard Hite, attorney-at-law. When he entered the outer room on the second floor, he was greeted by an attractive woman of middle years.

'Jed!' she exclaimed. 'What a nice surprise.'

Sloane bent down and kissed her. Instinctively, she looked about her.

'Don't worry,' Sloane said. 'There's nobody about. And even if there was, so what?'

She was still a little flustered but did not resist when he took her in his arms and kissed her again, hard on the lips.

'Now, tell Hite I want to see him,' he said.

She ran her hands over her skirt, then walked to a door behind her desk on which she knocked gently.

'What is it, Miss Chancellor?' a voice called.

'Someone to see you.'

'I'm busy at the moment.'

'It's Mr Sloane.'

There was movement from behind the door and then it was flung open.

'Jed! Come right on in.'

Sloane nodded to Miss Chancellor as he passed and she resumed her seat at the desk.

Hite's office was tastefully furnished and bore more of a resemblance to a study than an office. The man himself was tall and gangling, of about the same age as Sloane. He wore several large rings on his fingers and a maroon-coloured waistcoat.

'I didn't expect you in town today,' he said.

'Something came up,' Sloane replied.

Hite sat back in a leather chair and, taking a cigar, offered the box to Sloane, who took one. When they had clipped off the ends of the cigars and lit up, Sloane turned to the lawyer.

'I don't intend beating about the bush,' he said. 'Fact of the matter is, I had a meeting over breakfast this morning with Jackson Cook.'

Hite inhaled.

'He's more or less given me a deadline for getting Hethridge off the Lone Pine. That means I need you to give top priority to dealing with those papers.'

Hite nodded almost imperceptibly. 'I've got things under way,' he said.

'That's not good enough,' Sloane replied. 'Not now. I need you to give top priority to this. I want you to come up with whatever documentation it takes to prove Hethridge's title deeds to the Lone Pine are invalid. And quick.'

'That's easier said than done.'

'You're the lawyer. Get on with it. That is, if you still want your share of what this little enterprise is goin' to provide us with.'

Hite thought for a moment. 'I don't like being pressed,' he said.

'Like I say, get on with it or I'll find another lawyer.' Sloane got to his feet. 'Thanks for the cigar,' he said.

He moved to the door. Miss Chancellor made to rise as Sloane slammed through it but he strode past her without acknowledgment. He opened the outer door and was gone. She looked after his retreating figure until she was recalled to the present moment by the voice of Hite.

'Miss Chancellor. Could you come into my office? I have some urgent business and I shall need your assistance.'

★ ★ ★

A few days had gone by. Morgan Hethridge was standing by one of the corrals looking over the cattle that had been rounded up and brought in from the range. There were still a few old mossyheads waiting to be collected from the remoter draws and gullies and he had sent Brewer out with Riley to bring them in. This time, though, he had assigned a couple of his best hands to accompany them. Despite his concerns about the marshal, he had been pleased to see them ride back in, but thought it prudent to keep them out of the way.

So far the marshal had not returned but one of the hands, coming back from town, had reported seeing Wanted posters offering substantial rewards for the capture of Brewer and the oldster. Hethridge was a little puzzled by this. Why was the marshal so keen to bring them in and why was Sloane acting so provocatively? So far, apart from his discussion with Brewer, Riley had remained silent about his suspicions concerning the Plains & Western Company.

The cattle were now gathered in the corrals, where they had been left without food or water for a time to tame them down. When the time came to release them they would not immediately stampede into the brush. Hethridge knew the importance of this trail drive. The Eagle Creek bank was proving difficult and without the money the herd would bring in there was a chance the Lone Pine would go under. Now that the prairie was greening, Hethridge was keen to get started. Sloane's cattle were already on the hoof. He had a proposal to put to Brewer and the oldster when they got back that evening, that seemed to offer an answer to several of his difficulties.

It was dark by the time they got back, driving in a group of old stock that they had rousted out of the brush. It had been hard work but Brewer was pleased with the way the pinto had shaped up. He had proved to be a good cutting horse and willing to work.

'I figured ol' Flume to be a good 'un,' Riley said.

'I'd sure like to catch up with whoever left him to die in that swamp,' Brewer replied.

When they had corralled the cattle and tended their horses they made for the bunkhouse, where a broken piece of mirror glass hung over a trough of water and a battered bucket served for washing. Then they made their way to the ranch house. When they opened the door they were greeted by a warm aroma which set their taste buds tingling. The table was set with a blue checked tablecloth and napkins. To Brewer's consternation, Josie poked her head round the kitchen door.

'Father will be here directly,' she said. 'I thought you'd be a mite hungry after your day on the range so I've prepared a little something. Hope you like chicken.'

'Sure smells good,' Brewer said, taking off his hat and scrunching it awkwardly in his hands.

'Take a seat, it'll be ready soon.'

They hadn't been sitting for more than a few moments when Hethridge came down the stairs.

'Hello, gentlemen,' he said. He moved to a cabinet in a corner of the room. 'Whiskey?'

When they had enjoyed their drinks, Josie reappeared, carrying the plates of food.

'Won't you take a seat at the table?' Hethridge said. He smiled at her as she went out of the room.

'I don't know what I'd have done without her,' he remarked. 'She'll sure make someone a good wife.'

Riley glanced at Brewer, who was watching the retreating figure of the girl.

'Come on,' Hethridge said. 'Let's eat.'

When they had finished Hethridge poured some further drinks and offered them a cigar. They were feeling relaxed and comfortable. Hethridge drew in smoke, then breathed it out again.

'I wanted to see you gentlemen for a reason,' he began.

Brewer and Riley exchanged glances.

'As you know, the last of the cattle have just been rounded up. Having got to this stage, I don't want to delay. I won't go into details, but I'm sure that Brewer at least is aware of the delicate nature of the Lone Pine's finances. To be blunt, I need the money from this drive to see things through. That bein' the case, I need someone to take charge of the herd.'

'Won't that be Curly? He acted as trail boss last time,' Brewer said.

'I need Curly here. Nope, it's someone else I got in mind this time.'

Brewer looked puzzled. He turned to Riley again as if he might have the answer, then back to Hethridge.

'The person I'd like to take charge on this occasion is you,' Hethridge said.

Brewer's eyes opened wide in surprise. 'Me?' he said.

'If you feel you could handle it. I know it's a lot to ask. But I've watched you over the years and I figure you're just about ready to take on the responsibility.'

Brewer's face creased in a smile. 'Sure, Mr Hethridge,' he said. 'I'd be honoured to take it on. If you're sure it's me you want.'

Hethridge nodded. 'Since you came to the Lone Pine, you've been a real help to me. I know you're still a very young man, but I feel you're ready.'

Brewer didn't know what to say. 'I'd be honoured,' he repeated.

'Let's drink to it,' Hethridge said.

They tipped back their glasses, then Hethridge refilled them.

'Mr Riley,' he said. 'You seem to have struck up a good relationship with Brewer. I'd sure appreciate it if you'd agree to go along on this cattle drive too. There might be times when Brewer could do with a bit of advice and I understand you're an experienced hand in this business. How would you feel about that?'

Riley looked at Brewer and saw the keen look on the youngster's face.

'Mr Hethridge,' he said. 'I'm a hired hand. I'm just grateful that you took me on and gave me a job. It's my part to do whatever you tell me to.'

'Still, I'd like your agreement.'

'In that case I'd be plumb honoured too. And I appreciate you takin' the time to ask me like this.'

'Good. Then it's settled,' Hethridge said.

Riley looked thoughtful. 'Mr Hethridge,' he said. 'I hope you don't mind, but I feel I have some information that might be important to you. I wanted to mention it and now seems like as good a time as any.'

'Oh, and what's that?'

'I've already had a word with Brewer. It's just that I think there's more to this dispute between you and Jed Sloane than meets the eye and I think I know what it might be.'

While Brewer listened, Riley told Hethridge what he had learned about the Plains & Western Railroad's proposal to extend the railroad line and the implications it might have regarding Sloane's resolve to gain control of the Lone Pine. When he had finished Hethridge jumped to his feet and slammed the fist of his right hand into the palm of his left.

'I knew there was something goin' on,' he exclaimed. 'That explains it.'

He turned to the oldster. 'Mr Riley, I'm very grateful for this information. It seems I have even more cause to thank you. Your coming here is sure turning out to be a most fortunate occurrence.'

He stopped his perambulations and sat down again. 'Let me think about what you have told me. And in the meantime, I propose we take another drink to our enterprises.'

By the time they had swallowed another glass of the strong liquor Brewer's senses at least were a little befuddled. As he and Riley made their exits, for once he forgot to look out for Josie. If he had done so, he might have seen her at the top of the stairs with an expression on her features in which pride was mingled with concern and admiration.

* * *

The herd moved out early in the morning of the day following the next. Brewer, as the trail boss, rode ahead. To the eyes of Josie, looking out from her bedroom window, the cattle were an amorphous dark mass illumined here and there as a glint of light glanced off a horn or from the accoutrements of the riders. She watched until the figure of Brewer grew dim in the distance.

Gradually the cattle began to string out. Brewer raised himself in the saddle and looked back. He had charge of over 1,000 head of cattle and the men riding herd on them, and he felt the responsibility. Since he was a boy and Hethridge took him in he had been waiting for this. Now he meant to repay the trust that Hethridge had placed in him. Still, he was glad to have Riley along. His idea for the moment was to drive the herd hard the first couple of days in order to get them away from the home range and tire them so that when they were bedded down for the night they would be too weary to attempt to bolt. He had mixed a few old bulls with the herd to act as an example.

They set a steady pace. As he continued to survey the scene, he could see the two men who were riding point.

About a third of the way behind came the swing riders and behind them were the flankers. At the rear of the herd the drag riders were already obscured by dust. Off to the side the chuck wagon lumbered along and last of all came the wrangler with the remuda.

Towards noon the cattle were halted and allowed to graze, Brewer having found a good site without any sign of range stock which might distract the creatures. Before long they were on the trail once more and it was approaching dark before he signalled for the herd to be bedded down. He had found a good place with plenty of grass and water and a nice elevation on which the dry grass of the previous summer's growth provided a place for them to rest. Soon a few cows began to lie down and chew the cud. Others followed their example. The men continued to circle slowly round them till, within a short space of time, they were all bedded nicely, loose enough to give each animal room to turn or rise but tight enough for the night guards to be able to ride comfortably round the circle. The wrangler busied himself setting up a rope corral. Brewer had already observed that a few of the horses seemed skittish and so took the precaution of hobbling them. As he finished the task Whipcrack Riley approached him.

'That's good,' he said. 'I noticed one or two of those hosses strayin' from the bunch. Keep hazin' 'em back. They'll get the idea. We've made a good start. Give those cow critters another day or two and they'll be herd broke.'

The cattle had to be watched throughout the night, and the men took it in turns to do a shift of about two hours. Brewer had assigned himself and Riley to the cocktail watch. He turned in comparatively early to get some sleep, spreading his bedroll under the stars. Near by he could hear the muffled voices of the men still talking and, from further off, the bellowing of a cow rising on the evening breeze. The smell of cattle and horseflesh blended with the sweet scent of grass and flowers and the aroma of tobacco. Then he grabbed some sleep till it was time for him and Riley to take over the watch. As they circled the herd Riley's voice broke into a low hum.

'Loom up on 'em without singin' an' they'll be off at a lick,' the oldster explained.

Before the watch was over it was morning and the cattle were beginning to stir. The men made their way to the chuck wagon for breakfast but Brewer only had time to grab a mug of coffee. He would eat later. Accompanied by the wrangler, he went out to drive in the horses. They had grazed over a lot of ground and it took them some time. When they had got them all back, Brewer and the wrangler made their breakfast.

Brewer waited to throw the cattle off their bed-ground till some of the dew was off the grass. He didn't want the moisture to soften their hoofs. The cattle were slowly drifted and spaced far enough apart to keep them from standing on one another's heels. The men had caught and saddled their forenoon horses and the cattle were put in motion. Even as they grazed the men guided them so that they moved in the right direction. They continued in this way for two or three miles before being started on the trail.

In accordance with Brewer's desire to tire them and keep them docile they were driven four or five miles till noon. In starting out there was some initial confusion and a few of the longhorns caused trouble, but they were quieted down. At noon the cattle were allowed to drink. Some of the men changed their horses. Late in the afternoon the herd was again set in motion and driven another seven or eight miles till night was at hand, when they were grazed and then put on the next bedding ground. They were now well clear of the Lone Pine.

When Brewer awoke the next morning it was to find rain slanting in and most of the remuda scattered. He pulled on his slicker and saddled the pinto. The horses had drifted a good way across the prairie, but soon the men found them standing with their backs turned to the rain and their heads hanging. It didn't take long to round them up and begin to drive them back towards camp. The men had put on their slickers and pulled the brims of their hats low over their eyes as the rain lashed down and closed like curtains across the prairie.

Brewer had reminded the men about the increased danger of a stampede, but they needed no warning. Some of the cattle, agitated by the storm, began to stray to the side away from the rest of their fellows, and the swing and flank riders were kept busy patrolling up and down the herd. At the rear, Riley was assisting with the drag and the two drag riders were busy with their ropes, attempting to instil a bit of life into the weak and lazy cattle to stop them from falling behind. The cows were nervous and kept sniffing the air and the men were grateful that some of the leading older mossyhorns were unperturbed. They plodded on at their own steady pace, the rest of the herd following their example and treading in their wake.

It was a thoroughly miserable morning's work. Lightning continued to fork across the sky, but the storm appeared to be rolling away towards the west and by noon the rain had almost ceased. Brewer called a halt and the herd was allowed to graze. Taking advantage of the break, Riley approached him.

'You and Flume did a good job of roundin' up those hosses this mornin',' he said.

'The men did their bit.'

'Sure.' Riley ran his hands along the pinto's flanks.

'He makes a good night horse,' Brewer commented.

'Figure he'll make a good swimmin' hoss as well,' Riley replied. 'If there's rivers to cross up ahead.'

Soon after that they arrived at the first of them.

The rain had ceased, but the river was swollen. Brewer, together with Riley and Guthrie, observed it closely.

'There should be a ford at about this point,' Brewer said, 'but the river could be over the willows. Guthrie and me'll ride in and see how deep that water is. If there's swimmin' water, I want to know how much.'

When they were ready they spurred their horses down the riverbank, which was low at this point, and into the river. The men gathered on the bank raised a cheer. Hardly touching the reins, Brewer held the pinto's mane with one hand and gently slapped its neck with the other. He was whispering words of encouragement. The water came lapping over his boots and up the horse's flanks and was flowing quite quickly, but Flume's hoofs still seemed to rest on the bed of the river. Brewer could feel the horse straining against the pull of the current.

'OK?' he yelled to Guthrie.

'OK!' Guthrie shouted in return.

The water rose still further and Flume was swimming. The current carried them both a little way downstream but the horse was going well and in a few more seconds Brewer felt the change as its feet again found bedrock and they began to emerge from the water on the opposite side. Guthrie came up beside him, grinning and letting out a whoop. They dismounted and the dripping horses began to roll in the sand. A cheer rose from the opposite bank.

'Well,' Brewer said, 'I think we just about proved the crossing hereabouts. I guess we'd better cross back and start movin' the herd.'

When they rode back up the opposite bank Riley slapped Brewer across the back. He didn't need to say anything. About half the men were detailed to hold the cattle as compactly as possible while the other half crossed the river to receive them on the opposite side. A group of 250 head was cut out to make the first crossing. Brewer had put some of the leaders of the herd into the forefront to start the swim, but even so some of them began to balk at the prospect of crossing the water.

'Take the hosses across first,' Riley said.

The wrangler rode out with the remuda and with the help of the men eased them into the river. Behind them the cattle followed, some of the other riders swimming their horses on the downstream side to keep the herd from drifting. As they reached the deeper centre of the river, Brewer splashed water into Flume's face on the upstream side to help keep him going in the direction he wanted. The water was high but not turbulent and with the cowboys waving their hats and letting out a series of whoops and hollers, the cattle arrived safely at the opposite shore in the wake of the horses.

On landing some of the men held them close to the riverbank in order to bait the following bunch, and Brewer's horse again breasted the river as he struck for the other side to help guide the next batch of cattle across. When he was over he took the pinto over to the rope corral in order to rest him, and picked another horse, a sorrel with a similar barrel chest, indicating good swimming potential. Then, for the third time, he entered the stream.

His new horse did not seem to treat the water with the same ease and confidence as the pinto and on several occasions he came close to the cattle. However, he was still a good horse and swam without getting into any difficulties. Brewer had loosened the cinches and to keep him going in the right direction and not stray too far downstream he again splashed water into the horse's face on the upstream side.

So it went on without too much in the way of incident until about three quarters of the herd were across and they were about to make the final trip. Brewer was back on Flume as the group of cattle were started for the river. The leaders were close behind him as he moved into the water, the cowboys on the downstream side still guarding against any movement in that direction. They were approaching the middle of the stream when there came a cry from the bank:

'Floatin' log! Floatin' log!'

Brewer turned his head and saw the log coming down on the current. The lead cattle sensed something was wrong and started to move downstream. The men on that side attempted to keep them moving in a straight line for the opposite shore, but now a kind of panic began to spread through the herd and they started to mill. Instead of remaining in an orderly line, the cattle began to circle. Borne on the current, the log came hurtling along. Brewer urged the pinto forward and the horse responded, hitting the deeper water, but maintaining its impetus and not swerving out of line. The men, being downstream of the log, were protected by the cattle, but as Brewer's horse reached bedrock the log, narrowly missing Brewer, came crashing into the cattle.

They were swimming now in an ever tightening circle, but as the log smashed into them some of them went under; others broke away and the circle was partially broken. The men were attempting to break up the mass of panicking cattle and they were able to approach close to the centre of the mass. The log was deflected and went sideways, knocking into one horse's chest and unseating the rider. Down he went into the water, disappearing for a time, then bobbing up again further down in the centre of the river. Brewer became aware of Guthrie and Aldridge riding along the riverbank and into the water, where the man was struggling. Both of them leaped from their horses and surged into the river. Up on the bank another of the riders was swinging a lariat. It snaked out over the water and the man succeeded in catching it. By this time Guthrie and Aldridge had reached him and between them they were dragging the man out of the water to the safety of the riverbank. While they were doing this they narrowly missed being hit by the log themselves as it spun round again and continued its relentless journey down the river.

The circling of the cattle had slowed and now they were breaking up into smaller groups. One of the men had left his horse and crawled over the backs of a large group to get them turned. The others were riding amongst them, waving their hats in the faces of the cattle, and in some cases firing their guns close to the beasts to get them going in the direction they wanted. Brewer directed his horse to the wounded animal in the water and, seizing the reins, rode with it back to the riverbank. The herd was gradually being brought under control again, but just as Brewer thought the crisis was over there came the sound of shooting. Brewer glanced up to see groups of riders bearing down on them on both sides of the river. Choate!

Suddenly he realized that the incident with the log had been no accident: that they were under attack at just the point where they were at their most vulnerable. He dropped from the saddle and grabbed his rifle, slapping the pinto so that it moved away. Then he dived for the shelter of the riverbank. Lying flat, he drew a bead on the nearest rider and squeezed the trigger. The man flung out his arms and went tumbling from the saddle. There was a rattle of rifle fire from behind Brewer and he thought some of the attackers were coming from that direction. When he looked it was to see Guthrie and Aldridge blazing away. He turned his head to see what was happening on the far side of the river. The men there had taken what shelter they could and were also returning fire.

Cattle were still struggling across the river and, as a group of them were driven out of the water, Brewer couldn't suppress a grin to see the man who had crawled over the backs of the cattle emerge from the river hanging on to the tail of a confused longhorn. Brewer scrambled up the bank, took up a position and began to blaze away with his six-guns. The unseated man whom Guthrie and Aldridge had succeeded in dragging out of the river lay on the bank, still coughing and spluttering, but in a moment or two he seemed to have recovered sufficiently to get to his feet. Bent almost double, he ran after one of the loose horses and pulled a rifle from its scabbard. Then he pulled the horse to the ground and, taking shelter behind it, let loose a hail of lead.

Brewer looked up the river. Coming down on the current were more logs. They seemed to have got caught on some snag and were revolving slowly as they approached. Choate had probably intended to cause a lot more disruption but his plans had been foiled when the bulk of the logs got held back. A couple of other men had come up out of the river and with these reinforcements the struggle seemed to reach a turning point. The attackers drew to a halt and there was a brief discussion. Then they turned and began to ride away from the river, twisting and firing as they did so. Not having foreseen the situation with the logs, they had probably underestimated the strength of resistance they would meet. As far as Brewer could tell, the situation on this side of the river seemed to be under control, but what was happening on the other side?

He turned his head. There were more of the attackers over there and the battle was in full swing. The crack of gunfire echoed over the water and a cloud of smoke hung in the air. Brewer was considering whether to try and get across to help in the defence when the cattle still remaining on that side, goaded by the noise, began to turn and run.

In a moment Brewer could see that a miniature stampede was taking place, and that the cattle were moving in the direction of Choate's men. Realizing what was happening, they began to turn their horses but some of the scattered longhorns were already bearing down on them. Brewer stared hard but it was difficult to see exactly what was happening through the screen of dust and smoke. He heard screams as some of Choate's gunslicks went down under the trampling hoofs of the cattle but the scene was one of total confusion.

Some of the gunnies emerged from the mêlée riding hard to escape, and the continuing blasts of gunfire told Brewer it wasn't just the cattle they were running from. The first of the logs was now going past, catching some of the cattle which were still in the water. But Choate had been foiled. The logs had arrived too late.

Considering the mayhem caused by the one which had almost crashed into him earlier, Brewer could only heave a sigh of relief. He didn't know how many cattle he had lost and it would be a real job of work to recover the ones which had stampeded, but they had been lucky to come out of it at all. For the third time he and Riley had got the better of Choate and his gunnies, but would their luck hold?

Late that night, when the stray cattle had been rounded up and bedded down, Riley approached Brewer. The prairie lay dark beneath a cloudy sky and the only light visible was the lantern on the chuck-wagon. The nighthawks were circling the herd, and Brewer had assigned extra hands to the job in case of any further attack. However, he had a feeling that Choate would be unlikely to try anything again, especially as they were now ready for him. Choate had lost the advantage of surprise and was probably on his way back to the Buzzard On A Rail. And that thought was worrying him. As if he had caught something of Brewer's concern, Riley put down the mug of coffee he was drinking.

'It's a long ways to the railhead,' he said. 'Gonna take time.'

'Yeah.'

'A lot of time. Time we maybe ain't got.'

Brewer looked across at the oldster. 'How do you mean?' he said.

'Look at it this way,' Riley said. 'We both know why Hethridge put us down for this ride.'

'The herd has to be sold,' Brewer replied.

'Yeah, but he was really thinkin' of the marshal and gettin' us out of the way. Same reason he sent us off to the line cabin.'

'Maybe so.'

'He had other reasons. One of them was to see how you would shape up. Well you done enough already to convince anyone who needed convincin' that you're more than ready for the job. Hell, I seen you take charge of this outfit. I seen how you handle the cow critters and the way you have with the hosses. The men are right behind you. You don't need to prove yourself any further.'

Brewer looked slightly embarrassed and shrugged his shoulders.

'The way I figure it, if you decided to head back for the ranch nobody would think any less of you. You could appoint either Guthrie or Aldridge to take over as trail boss. Either of 'em would make a good job of it.'

'And why would I do that?'

'Because you're thinkin' twice about the whole thing. You're worryin' about what might be happenin' back at the ranch. Things there is buildin' to a head and that's where you want to be, not here. You're thinkin' that that's where you might really be needed and I agree.'

Brewer picked up his coffee mug and took another swig.

'I'm thinkin' the same,' Riley said. 'I been thinkin' about what Drewitt had to say about the Plains and Western and it seems to me that Drewitt is in a lot more trouble even than he realizes. He done me a good turn takin' me on as driver when my luck was down. I figure I owe him.'

Brewer got to his feet and began to walk about. Then he squatted down beside the oldster.

'You're right,' he said. 'I been thinkin' about the Lone Pine ever since we started out. I figure things are a lot worse than I realized. I don't know exactly what it is, but somethin's got me plumb worried.'

'I figure our place is back there,' Riley said. 'The boys here can handle the rest of the drive. I say we start headin' back first thing tomorrow.'

Brewer paused. 'What do I tell the boys?' he said.

The oldster grinned. Brewer was not much more than a boy himself but he had shown his mettle.

'Tell 'em the truth,' he replied. 'They'll understand.'

The next morning, after Brewer had explained his concerns and the cattle had been set in motion, Brewer and Riley turned their horses in the direction of the Lone Pine.

4

At the stage depot in Rock Corner there was pandemonium. The stage from Eagle Creek had come under fire and the shotgun guard had been killed.

'This is the second time this has happened,' the driver said. 'I'm sorry, Mr Drewitt, but I quit.'

He didn't waste any time in argument but turned on his heels and walked away. The body of the guard had been lifted down and lay in a back room of the stage depot. He had been killed by a single shot to the head. When the undertaker arrived, he whistled and turned to Drewitt.

'Mighty neat piece of shootin',' he said. 'How did it happen?'

'Someone fired on the stage from ambush.'

'Like I say, as neat a shot as I've seen.

And you say it was from a distance and the gun was aimed at a moving target?'

'Seems that way,' Drewitt said.

In the main office people were milling around. An elderly lady sat on a chair while someone was administering smelling salts. Another woman was sobbing gently and being comforted by a black-suited gentleman and a young boy. At that moment the marshal came in. Drewitt approached him.

'What are you goin' to do about it this time?' he said. 'The same thing happened last week and I don't see much in the way of action.'

The marshal looked him over. 'I'm doin' what I can,' he said. 'I've contacted my counterpart in Eagle Creek and we'll be workin' on it together.'

Drewitt laughed. 'That would be Marshal Burke. If you're plannin' on workin' with him, you might as well go straight to the top.'

'What do you mean?'

'Some folks reckon he's frontin' for Jed Sloane. And Jed Sloane's the very man would do best out of bankruptin' the stage line.'

'What are you tryin' to imply?'

Drewitt shook his head. 'I ain't implyin' nothin', Marshal,' he said. 'You just try thinkin' about it.'

The marshal looked at Drewitt with a hostile glint in his eye. Drewitt turned on his heel.

'I ain't got time to stand here arguin' with you,' he said. 'Right now I got a stagecoach due to leave for Lansberg in half an hour and nobody to drive it.'

Morning broke over the Lone Pine. Things had been quiet since Brewer had left on the trail drive and Josie was missing him. She woke after a restless night with the sunlight streaming over her bedspread. She got out of bed, went across to the stables, saddled her horse and set off for a ride. She had been feeling unhappy since Brewer's departure but as she urged the Appaloosa gelding into a brisk trot she began to feel her spirits lift. It was a glorious day. The sun was already gaining in strength but a fresh breeze stirred the grass, little white cloudlets floated in the sky and there was a freshness about the atmosphere that still bore the tang of the recent rains. The pastures were strangely empty now that the cattle had been rounded up, so it was with something of a surprise that she saw a group of three riders in the distance. She stopped the Appaloosa and drew a pair of binoculars from a saddle-bag. The riders were not anyone she recognized. She replaced the binoculars and urged her horse forward again. She was feeling a little uneasy but carried on riding in the direction she had been going, fighting back an urge to start heading back towards the ranch.

When she looked again, the riders had turned and seemed to be coming in her direction. Her unease was increased and she touched her spurs to the horse's flanks. She was a good rider and she was astride a good horse. She felt sure that she could outride the group of horsemen, but why would she be thinking in those terms? She took another glance and the riders were definitely closer. Not bothering to think any further about it, she urged the gelding into a gallop.

The horse responded and in a few moments it was bounding across the prairie. She let it have its head, and when she looked back she could see no trace of the riders. There was a rise in the ground between her and where they should be, so she couldn't be sure whether they were still there or not. Not far ahead of her a stand of trees indicated where the Deep Fork took a turn; she rode her horse into the trees and down into the stream. She rode along it a little way, then she turned back and retraced her steps. The horse splashed through the shallow water till it reached a spot where a little brook came down through a draw. She knew the spot. It was where she sometimes used to come when she was younger, a secret spot that she would come to when she wanted to be alone and leave the affairs of the ranch behind her.

There was no obvious trail up through the brush, but she turned the Appaloosa off along the brook and then up the bank into some trees until she reached the place she was looking for, an open space overlooking the brook where a leaning, broken branch provided a place for her to sit. She dismounted and tied the horse. She moved to the tree branch but, instead of using it as a seat, as was her wont, she climbed along it till she reached a point where she could reach up to another branch and, with a little exertion, swing up into the foliage. From there she had a decent view of the brook to its junction with the Deep Fork while being concealed herself.

Out of a pocket of her riding breeches she drew a double-barrelled pocket pistol. Holding it carefully, she prepared to wait. She still couldn't have said exactly why she had taken the action she had or what she feared, but it didn't take long for her suspicions to be confirmed. First she heard the sound of splashes and then the snicker of a horse. Glancing down, she looked towards the Appaloosa to ensure that she had hidden its whereabouts. What if it should give her away by making a sound? What if it was disturbed by the presence of the other three horses? There was nothing she could do but hope and pray that the Appaloosa would not give her away.

A short time later the three riders came into view. Her first feeling was one of disappointment that her ruse of doubling back on herself had apparently failed; then her attention was fully occupied with the scene below. Just before they reached the point where the brook ran into the Deep Fork, the riders brought their horses to a halt and she was able to observe them more closely. Her intuition had been correct and she had been right to take precautionary measures. The three men were unshaven, mean-looking and well armed. They certainly didn't look like the usual type of ranch hand although their horses, when her eyes focused, bore the Buzzard On A Rail brand.

'Maybe she went the other way after all,' one of them remarked.

'Maybe. I don't think so.'

'What do you think, Lannigan? Do we carry on?'

The man referred to as Lannigan seemed to be the leader of the group. He wore a black leather waistcoat over a red shirt, and unlike the other two his head was bare and shaved close. He raised himself in the saddle and took a look around. Josie's heart gave a thump as for a moment he seemed to stare straight at her, but then his glance moved away.

'Pity Choate ain't here,' he said. 'I figure he would sure appreciate comin' on that little filly.'

The others laughed.

'He sure has the hots for her,' one of them commented. 'Can't say I blame him. She sure is a pretty one.'

'You better not let Choate hear you

say anythin' like that.'

'No way,' the man said. 'I'll settle for a trip to the Bull Run on payday.'

'Still, I figure Choate would be mighty grateful if we were to rope the filly for him.'

'What about Sloane?'

'Sloane wouldn't mind. In fact, I got a feelin' he'd have no objections at all.'

'Thing is,' the first man retorted, 'where's she gone now?'

'She can't be far,' Lannigan replied. 'I reckon we carry on this way, at least for now.'

Suiting action to his words, he spurred his horse forward and the three riders carried on down the stream. Josie watched till they were out of sight and only then felt able to breathe freely. She discovered that she was trembling. Taking in deep breaths of air, she leaned back against the trunk of the tree and considered what she should do next.

★ ★ ★

When Brewer and Riley rode into the yard of the Lone Pine they were surprised when the door of the ranch house burst open and Hethridge came running down the steps.

'I don't know what you boys are doin' here,' he said, 'but I sure am glad to see you.'

Brewer slid from the saddle. 'Why, what's happened?'

'Maybe nothin', but I'm startin' to get worried.'

'Worried about what, Mr Hethridge?' Riley said.

'It's Josie. She went off this mornin' and she ain't been seen since.'

'Miss Josie!' Brewer gasped.

'Take it steady,' Riley said. 'Let's hear Mr Hethridge out before jumpin' to conclusions.'

'Riley's right,' Hethridge said. 'I'm probably makin' a fuss out of nothin'. After all, it's perfectly normal for her to take a ride and quite often she takes her time about gettin' back. I don't know why I'm actin' this way. I guess it's just the way things have been recently, what with the attack on Brewer and all. Here, come inside and we'll talk about it.'

When they had gone inside and Hethridge had spoken further, Brewer couldn't hide his agitation.

'Let's get ridin',' he said. 'Where does Miss Josie normally go? We should be able to pick up her trail.'

'Just calm down,' Hethridge said. 'Josie's a sensible girl. She can look after herself. She ain't been gone much longer than normal. Just wait a bit longer and she'll come ridin' in. In the meantime, you ain't said just what you're doin' back here. Is there some sort of trouble with the herd?'

Brewer started to speak but his thoughts were obviously elsewhere and Riley took up the story. He tended to gloss over the matter of the attack on the herd by the river crossing, but even so Hethridge was ablaze with anger.

'If Choate was involved, then you can be sure it was the Buzzard On A Rail behind it,' he ranted. 'It's about time I really had it out with that varmint Sloane.'

'We got no proof that Choate was involved,' Riley commented.

'You don't mean that,' Brewer said.

'OK, so it was almost certainly Choate. But even so, we don't know that he was actin' under orders. The polecat may be in the pay of the Buzzard On A Rail, but Sloane seems to have a slim hold on him.'

Brewer got to his feet and began to walk up and down the room.

'I'm sorry,' he said, 'but I can't just stand here talkin' any longer while Miss Josie may be in danger. I got to do somethin'.'

Hethridge regarded him with a sympathetic eye.

'OK,' he said. 'I'm beginnin' to feel the same. I'll come with you.'

'I appreciate that, but I reckon it might be better if I went alone. I could make quicker time that way.'

Hethridge thought for a moment before reluctantly agreeing.

'I guess someone should be here in case she makes her own way back. After all, it's probably a storm in a teacup.'

'What about you?' Brewer said to Riley.

'You two can handle things,' Riley said. 'Right now I reckon I got some business in Eagle Creek.'

'What sort of business?' Brewer said.

'You remember what we were sayin' about the stage line and the Plains and Western? Well, I reckon I got something important to discuss with Jim Drewitt.'

* * *

Josie Hethridge remained up the tree for a long time before even considering the possibility of coming down again. Although she was a brave and self confident woman, what she had seen of the men pursuing her had left her frightened and unsettled. What she had heard of their conversation convinced her that she could expect little consideration at their hands. It looked like they might be out to kidnap her and, if she remembered correctly, Choate was the name of one of the men who had tried to lynch Brewer. How she wished that Brewer would come by, that he could be with her now.

When she was reasonably sure that the riders would not return, she carefully shifted her position so that she could begin to climb down from the tree. Careful as she was, however, when she turned to face the tree and placed her foot on the next branch, she felt it slip. She made a desperate grab at the branch above but her hand slipped away, grasping only a handful of twigs and leaves. The next moment she lost her balance completely and came crashing down through the intervening branches, landing heavily and bashing her head against the base of the tree. She lay inert while the tethered horse shifted uneasily.

When she came round she didn't know where she was. She was lying on her side and her neck and shoulders were aching. She also had a bad headache and her foot hurt. Her head was twisted round where she had landed awkwardly but she succeeded in moving it and then in raising herself so that she was lying with the upper part of her back against the tree bole. When she tried to get to her feet, however, she fell back with a gasp. Something was wrong with her ankle. She tried again but the stab of pain that shot through her foot persuaded her that to stand upright was out of the question. She had either sprained or broken her left ankle.

Braving the pain in her neck, she turned her head towards where she had tied the horse, in order to calculate the distance she would have to slither to get to it. The horse was gone. When she could not see it, she grew frightened. Maybe the riders had come back and found it. But then they would have found her too, even though she was concealed in the tree. Somehow it must have slipped its rein. She gave a groan in which pain and disappointment were mingled.

What was she to do now? She couldn't move, or at least not very far and only with the greatest difficulty. She was hungry and thirsty and the night was coming on. Unless someone found her, she was helpless. And who would be likely to find her in the secret place she had specifically selected for the security it offered? Night descended swiftly in the shade of the trees and she began to feel cold. Adjusting her riding habit to make best use of the warmth it provided, she lay down and her eyes closed.

★　★　★

When Calvin Choate returned to the Buzzard On A Rail, he was not particularly well received. Once again he had failed to come up with the goods and Sloane was not pleased.

'We ran off most of the herd,' Choate lied. 'Brewer will be hard put to make it the rest of the way without the men we killed.'

'If you took out so many, how come you didn't stay to finish the job?'

'We figured it'd be best to get back here.'

Sloane was exasperated. 'You'd better not fail me again,' he rapped.

'Just say what you want and I'll get it done,' Choate replied.

Sloane was thinking. At least Brewer was out of the way and some damage had been inflicted on the chances of the Lone Pine raising the cash they needed. He could even have another word with Marshal Burke and see if he could arrange for a posse to ride out and collect Brewer. Right now events were speeding up and it might be useful to have Choate on hand. It was a pity he had to take people like Choate into his employ but it couldn't be helped. It was just unfortunate that Choate appeared to be so incompetent. Maybe that wouldn't matter so much if he put him on to something that required much more in the way of sheer brawn than any job he had assigned him to so far.

'Do you think you could manage with a shovel?' he said.

'A shovel. How do you mean?'

'Just a little something I've thought of that might help convince Hethridge that he's be better off sellin' up than tryin' to make a show of things with the Lone Pine.' Choate looked blank. 'I've already got some of the boys involved.'

'Involved in what?'

Sloane looked the slobbery figure of the gunman up and down.

'Guess you could do with the exercise. It's like this. The Lone Pine relies on the Deep Fork for its water supply. Part of it runs through Buzzard On A Rail land. If we block it up, the Lone Pine's out on a limb.'

Choate seemed to struggle with the idea.

'Like I say, some of the boys have already started work on it. Regular little team of beavers,' Sloane said. 'Take a few of the men who've just come back with you and get yourselves down there.'

Suddenly Choate's eyes lit up. 'I got it!' he said.

'Got what?'

'Dynamite!' Choate replied. 'I used to work with the stuff. It was a whiles ago but I remember how to handle it.'

Sloane looked dubious.

'A few sticks of dynamite would come in mighty useful blockin' off that stream,' Choate said. 'I seen it done before at the diggin's.'

It was something Sloane had not considered, but as he thought about it the idea seemed to make some kind of sense.

'If you're sure you know what you're doing,' he said to Choate.

'Leave it to me, boss. This'll sure speed things up some.'

At a signal from Sloane that the discussion was ended Choate turned on his heels and went out through the door. Watching him go, Sloane wasn't quite so sure. Well, he thought, what does it matter so long as they get the job done? Following Choate, he made for the stables, where his horse was waiting ready saddled, and started off in the direction of town.

The lawyer, Everard Hite, was expecting Sloane's visit and was prepared for his arrival. He heard the rancher come up the stairs, then there was a brief interlude. That will be him carrying on with Miss Chancellor, Hite thought. In another few moments the secretary knocked on the door and Sloane was admitted.

'Nice to see you, Mr Sloane. Please take a seat.'

Sloane sat down. 'Well,' he rapped. 'Have you got those documents prepared?'

'Just about. Paperwork's almost done.'

'I told you I wanted it done pronto.'

'Mr Sloane, I'm doing my best. You must realize that these things take time.'

'I ain't got time. Either those documents are ready by noon tomorrow or you're out of the deal.'

A slight lifting of the corners of his mouth indicated that Hite was smiling. Or was it a gesture of distaste?

'As I say, these things take a little time. Just be patient a little longer. However, I do have something to report.'

'Yeah? And what might that be?'

'My researches have led me to examine the title deeds of several of the properties in the area and something very interesting has emerged.'

'Get on with it.'

'Well, to put it bluntly, Mr Sloane, there seems to be some query about your own title deeds to the Buzzard.'

Sloane did not move but Hite could see that the bolt had gone home. There was a lengthy pause.

'I don't know what you mean,' Sloane said.

'It's quite simple. It appears that the property once belonged to a gentleman named Hayes. He died some time ago, in fact about the same time as you came to Eagle Creek. There were some suspicious circumstances associated with his death, but nothing ever came of them.'

'What are you trying to insinuate?'

'Absolutely nothing. But some people at the time apparently found it a little curious that the Buzzard On A Rail found its way into your hands. After all, so far as people could tell, neither of you even knew the other.'

Sloane got to his feet. 'I've had enough of this,' he barked. 'I don't know what your game is, Hite, but I'd advise you to be very careful about what you say. In fact, if I were you I'd watch my next step very closely. Do you understand me?'

'If I've disturbed you in any way, then I apologize. However, things are as they are. If sleeping dogs are to be left where they lie, then there may be a cost involved.'

'Just have those documents ready next time I stop by.' Sloane paused and looked Hite in the eye. 'I don't take kindly to threats,' he added.

Hite's grin grew just a little wider. It was a nervous gesture.

'I'm sure I don't know what you're getting at,' he replied. 'Let's put it this way. The fees for my services have just increased. By a substantial amount.'

Sloane emitted something between a snarl and a laugh.

'You'll get just whatever you're due,' he said.

For the second time in consecutive visits Miss Chancellor was ignored as he stormed past her desk and out of the door.

Jim Drewitt was sitting in his office at the stage depot in Eagle Creek, feeling more than a little worried. Because of the attacks on the stagecoaches he was finding it almost impossible to find drivers. Two guards had been killed. There had been no stages between Eagle Creek, Rock Corner and Lansberg for three days and it looked like the line was about to fold. He had been holding off bids from the Plains & Western Railroad Company for a considerable time because they were way below what he figured the stage line was worth, but now it looked like he might be forced out of business altogether. He poured a stiff glass of whiskey from the bottle which stood on his desk and looked out of the back window at the two scarlet Concord coaches standing idly in the yard. They had cost him over $1,000 each and he still owed the bank. Just then a shadow appeared in the open doorway and next moment someone entered. He couldn't see at first who it was because of the sunlight but as the man came forward, he recognized with sudden pleasure the face of his old friend Whipcrack Riley.

'Whipcrack!' he exclaimed. He jumped to his feet and seized Whipcrack by the hand. 'What are you doin' back in these parts?'

'Workin' for a spread called the Lone Pine.'

'Morgan Hethridge's place? How come you wound up there?'

'It's a long story,' Riley replied.

'I reckon you could put away a drink,' Drewitt commented.

Riley looked at the half empty bottle and then at his friend. 'Sure could,' he said.

Drewitt got a glass and poured him a drink. While he did so Riley looked out of the window and saw the coaches standing in the yard.

'Business not so good?' he queried.

'Worst it's ever been. Couple of guards been shot recently and nobody wants to take on the job, either drivin' or ridin' messenger.'

'That's a mite unusual,' Riley said. 'I can't remember exactly how long I was drivin' those contraptions, but I don't remember havin' no trouble.'

'You're right,' Drewitt replied. 'I can't seem to figure it out.'

Riley took a long swig of whiskey. 'How long's it been goin' on?'

'The shootin'? Just this last couple of weeks. But there were little incidents before that. Nothin' much but enough to cause me a few headaches. Wheel come loose, horse goin' lame, that sort of thing.'

131

'Just coincidence?'

'I don't know. I thought so but now I'm beginnin' to wonder. The stage line just seems to be cursed.'

Riley drank again. 'What you say don't really surprise me,' he said.

Drewitt looked up.

'Last time I was drivin' for you, you happened to mention the Plains & Western Railroad Company. At that time there was just some vague talk about them maybe buildin' a spur line out this way. Now I gather it's more definite. If you don't mind me askin', what are they offerin' you for the stage company?'

'Not enough,' Drewitt replied. 'I don't want to sell up anyway, but I'm old enough to know which way the wind is blowin'. There's no holdin' back progress. But I'd like to be paid a fair amount for the company. I'm only askin' what it's worth.'

'And they're offerin' a lot less. Have you thought that maybe they figure the time has come to put more pressure on you?'

Drewitt's brows contracted in thought. 'Funny you should say that,' he said. 'I guess I hadn't got round to seein' things in quite that way, but now you mention it, I was beginnin' to wonder if there might be somethin' more involved.'

'Look,' Riley said, 'let me tell you exactly what I think is goin' on.'

In a few words he outlined what Brewer had told him of what he knew about the situation between the Lone Pine and the Buzzard On A Rail and the things which had been taking place recently.

'My guess is that Sloane and the Plains & Western are in cahoots. They're puttin' pressure on anybody who stands in their way. At first it was little things but now that the stakes are higher, they're pilin' it on more. Sloane wants to get his hands on the Lone Pine because of the right of way. The Plains & Western offer him a bargain price and even so he cleans up. The railroad gets the land rights. Everyone's a winner.'

'Except for me and Morgan Hethridge,' Drewitt exclaimed. He looked angrily at Riley. 'You figure the Plains and Western are behind the killin's of my employees?'

'Who's behind the Plains and Western?' Riley asked.

'A man by the name of Jackson Cole.'

Riley grinned. 'Now ain't that a surprise?' he said. 'If he's the same Jackson Cole used to be involved with the Lone Mountain Railroad scandal that would sure fit.'

'Lone Mountain?' Drewitt said.

'It was to do with the hire of Chinese labour in the Sierras. Nasty business.'

The two men were silent for a moment.

'Anyway,' Riley remarked, 'it don't matter much exactly whose pullin' the strings, whether it's Sloane or Cole or whatever combination, the outcome is the same.'

Drewitt poured another drink. 'Is that why you came to see me?' he said. 'If so, what are you proposin'?'

'I want my job back,' Riley said.

Drewitt laughed. 'Sure,' he said, 'it's yours. I only wish I could find a few others the same.'

Riley had risen to his feet and now looked out of the window. Down the street he could see Marshal Burke walking towards the stage depot.

'Drewitt,' he said, 'I gotta leave. Don't worry, I'll be back in touch real soon.'

'Where are you goin'?'

'Marshal's goin' to be here in a minute. I don't want him to see me. Is there a back way out?'

Drewitt peered out at the street, then grinned. 'Sure,' he said. 'Right this way.'

Together they went through a door which led into a back office. Another door took them outside to where a number of horses stood in the corrals and the two stagecoaches gathered dust. Drewitt pointed with his finger to a fence, behind which were some trees.

'Thanks,' Riley said. 'Be seein' you real soon.'

Drewitt watched him as he awkwardly climbed the fence and set off into the trees.

'Now I wonder what else the old buzzard has been up to?' he said to himself and then went back inside to face the marshal.

Once he had reached the shelter of the trees Riley came to a halt. He had intended making his getaway but now a sudden thought struck him. He stood for a while regaining his breath while he considered the new idea which had occurred to him. Maybe he could kill two birds with one stone. It depended on just how open to reason the marshal might be. He, Riley, would be putting himself at some risk if he was to put his idea to the test. He started to move away through the trees before coming to a stop again. Then he turned and began to retrace his steps, making his way to the marshal's office to await Burke's return.

★ ★ ★

When Brewer set off from the Lone Pine in search of Josie he was in such a state of turmoil that he failed to recognize any sign of her as he rode across the range. One thing he was certain of: when he found her and she was safe he would lose no more time in letting his feelings be known to her. It didn't matter if his case was hopeless, if she was too far above him. At least the burden of keeping it to himself would be lifted.

He rode hard at first and then, as his first sense of outrage and anxiety began to subside, he slowed the pinto to an easy trot and began to look around him. He had been travelling in the direction of the Buzzard On A Rail and as he calmed down he realized that this was probably the wrong way to go. If Josie had set off for a ride, she would be more likely to follow the line of the Deep Fork. He turned his horse and set off in that direction.

He rode for some time without seeing anything, then his eyes picked out something a little way off to his right. When he rode up he found obvious sign that three riders had passed that way. There was nothing particularly unusual in that but for some reason he felt suspicious. The cattle were gone and there was no need for anyone to be riding through. The Lone Pine hands were pretty well accounted for. Could that mean that the riders were from the Buzzard On A Rail? In which case they were trespassing on Lone Pine property. Having no other plan in mind, he decided to follow their trail.

It was easy to track. After a while it took a sudden turn and when he got down to examine the sign more closely he could tell that the horses had broken into a gallop at that point. Why would they have done that? He remounted the pinto and started off again. The trail was leading him in the general direction of the Deep Fork and eventually he saw trees ahead indicating the course of the stream. The tracks led straight through the trees and into the water. He looked up and down the stream, looking for clues. He rode a little way and then some bent leaves on a willow leaning into the water told him that the riders had probably passed that way.

Glancing carefully from side to side, he carried on riding, the splashing sound of his horse's hoofs mingling with the rustle of leaves in the breeze. Before long he came to a spot where a brook ran into the main stream. Bringing the pinto to a halt, he looked about him for clues as to where to go next. There seemed to be no route leading up into the trees from the brook and he decided to carry on along the stream. Whispering gently, he urged Flume forward.

Only a matter of yards away the unconscious body of Josie lay where she had fallen from her tree.

5

At a point not too far from where the property of the Lone Pine merged into the Buzzard On A Rail, a gang of Buzzard hands were busily employed in damming up the Deep Fork when Calvin Choate arrived on the scene. The saddlebags on the horse he was riding were bulging with something and when Choate dismounted and began unpacking sticks of dynamite most of the men stood back while others moved even further away.

'It's OK,' Choate said. 'Nothin' can happen till they been primed.'

'Sure you know what you're doin?' one of the man said.

'Look, Clem, I've had experience with this sort of thing.'

He looked over the work the men had done. 'Gonna save you all a lot of back-breakin' toil,' he said. 'What

140

you're doin' is a fool's way to block this damn river.'

The leader of the group, a man named Seth Jones, looked unconvinced.

'Dynamite seems a mite crude to my way of thinkin',' he said. 'The way we're doin' it might be slow but it's quite a delicate business. The Lone Pine is one thing. We don't want to cause no problems for the Buzzard. What happens if we do somethin' to affect our water supply?'

Choate gave him a withering glance.

'Like I say, if you boys want to carry on breakin' your backs, then go right on ahead.'

The men looked at one another. They had no liking for the job they were doing. Anything which offered them the chance of getting back in the saddle was worth consideration.

'You sure you got Sloane's approval for this?' Jones enquired.

'Sure. Now if you'll just give me space, I'll have this riverbank blasted out in no time.'

The men laid down their shovels. Choate unpacked the rest of his dynamite and began to poke at the muddy walls of the riverbank.

'Somebody lend a hand!' he shouted. 'I need someone with a pick.'

The men exchanged glances.

'Come on! I need to dig holes into the bank.'

There was a marked lack of response before Jones stepped forward.

'Like Clem said, I sure hope you know what you're doin,' he remarked.

Choate showed him where to dig the holes he needed in order to insert the sticks of dynamite. As he dug each one Choate cut one of the sticks and inserted it into the hole. When five holes had been dug and filled in this way, Choate ordered Jones to stand back. Quickly, Jones ran to join the others where they were cowering at what they hoped was a safe distance behind any cover they could find.

Choate slipped a cap on to each of the five sticks of dynamite, lit the fuses, and ran towards the others. He had got about halfway when suddenly, with an almighty roar, the riverbank erupted. Rocks and mud and parts of trees flew into the air and came raining down while the running figure of Choate was outlined against a blinding flash of light. He flung up his arms and fell forward as a shower of debris came raining down from the sky upon him and the others. The men lay flat, their ears ringing from the boom of the explosion, till gradually one and then another began to raise their heads.

Between them and the stream a dense cloud of smoke hung in the air and drifted towards them. Choate lay on the grass, not moving. Presently Jones felt sufficiently confident to stagger to his feet and move forward, shaking his ringing head and tugging at his ears. Behind him the others started to stir. Stumbling forward, Jones reached the inert form of Choate. He feared Choate was dead. Kneeling beside him, he raised the dusty figure and turned him over. The man lay limp in his arms and his eyes were closed. Just as Jones was about to lay him on the ground his eyes opened and he looked up. Blood ran from his nostrils and his face was black and grimy. Gradually a thin smile twitched the corners of his mouth.

'What did I tell you?' he said. 'Sure beats diggin' a dam the hard way.'

Jones laid him down and moved through the smoke towards the river. He could still hear a sound of flowing water and when he reached what had been the bank of the stream it was to find it blown away. Almost as if by magic, the explosion seemed to have released a torrent of running water further upstream. The Deep Fork had been quite shallow at this point but the destruction of the riverbank had apparently caused a surge.

Further down he could see that other parts of the bank had crumbled beneath the added pressure and at places where the bank was low the water had flooded into the surrounding fields. A cascade of debris had created a kind of small island in the middle of the river, around which the waters broke and separated into two before joining up again. But where they met they had been reduced to a trickle. Jones turned away as the others came alongside him. Bringing up the rear was the sorry figure of Choate.

'I told you boys,' he was mouthing. 'I know how to handle dynamite. You'll be grateful now for the work I've saved you.'

★   ★   ★

Night descended as Brewer worked his way up the streambed. Although his instincts were driving him to continue, the rational part of him realized the pointlessness of continuing any further and he began to look about for a suitable place to camp. He tugged on the reins and the pinto rode up the shallow bank and into the trees.

When he emerged into the open the first thing he saw was a faint glow in the distance. It could only be a campfire. He guessed it was the riders whose trail he had crossed. He also surmised they were from the Buzzard On A Rail. What were they doing out here? The country between where they were and the town of Lansberg was rough and inhospitable. Only a section of the stagecoach route ran through it.

Thinking of the stagecoach made him think of Riley. What was he doing with Drewitt? His thoughts turned back to Josie. His first impulse was to ride into the camp and simply ask if they had seen anything of her. Then he thought of the near hanging he had received at the hands of other Buzzard riders and he thought better of it. Better creep up on them and investigate.

He rode a little further and then, fearing that he might be seen or that the pinto might give him away, he dismounted and, after hobbling the horse,

146

crept forward on foot. The camp was in a little hollow which made his approach easier. When he had reached a position where he could see into the camp and hear what the men were saying, he drew his six-gun and lay flat. The words the men were speaking sounded remarkably clear. The breeze was blowing in Brewer's direction and he didn't need to strain his ears to pick up what they were saying.

'That little filly has got to be hidin' somewhere by the river. I say we got plenty of time to head on back there in the mornin'.'

There was the sound of a low laugh. 'Forget her, Johnson. She was only a sideshow, after all. We got other business to attend to.'

'I figure Choate might have some-thin' to say if'n you tried anythin' with that piece of petticoat. He reckons he's gonna have her some day.'

Brewer had tensed. The filly they were referring to could only be Josie. At least she was not in their control. His instinctive reaction was to creep away, find his horse and go back to resume the search, but something told him to wait a little longer and see if he could discover any further information. One of the men threw a stick on to the fire and glanced away into the night. For a moment Brewer stiffened as the man's eyes searched in his direction. He flattened himself against the ground but the moment of tension passed as the man turned back to his fellows.

'Talkin' about Choate, I hope he knows more about what he's doin' when it comes to range calico than he does when it comes to finishin' off a boy and an oldster,' someone said.

'Choate's a rogue buffalo. It don't do to cross him.'

'Choate's under orders, same as us. If Sloane reckons we need to stay out here to attack the next stage, I guess we ain't got much choice.'

'The stage is out of action.'

'At the moment. Sloane wants to be sure he's got all the angles covered.'

There was a mutter of dissension from another man. 'And meantime we just got to kick our heels waitin' for a stage that probably won't come. I reckon we'd do better to find the girl. Hell, we'd have somethin' to occupy ourselves with then.'

Brewer guessed the speaker was the man named Johnson. He gritted his teeth.

'Like I say, forget about the girl.'

'I don't get it. Sloane's after the Lone Pine. Why's he botherin' with the stage at all?'

'It's part of the same thing. The stage company and the Lone Pine are the two things standin' between him and a fortune. The more he leans on 'em both, the better chance he has of comin' out on top.'

'And what about us? What do we get out of it at the end of the day?'

'He's payin' well. That's all you need to worry about.'

Brewer had heard enough. Being careful not to make a sound, he began to slither away. It was not an easy process as his damaged shoulder began to give him trouble, but he soon felt able to get fully to his feet. The pinto was where he had left it and he stepped into the saddle. He wheeled round and began to retrace his steps.

If the Buzzard riders had been in pursuit of Josie, she must be somewhere between where he was now and the place he had first picked up their trail. The likeliest place she would have chosen to hide would be somewhere back along the river. He rode through the trees and into the water. He wished it was daylight so he could see better but the sky was clear and there was light enough. After a time he began to call Josie's name, straining his ears for any reply. After a time the pinto's head came up. His ears were pricked.

'What is it, Flume?' Brewer whispered.

The horse was perturbed by something and when he came round a slight bend Brewer realized what it was.

Standing on the edge of the water was a horse, fully saddled. Brewer slid down and approached it. Although he didn't know exactly which horse Josie rode, he knew it was hers and it carried the Lone Pine brand. Now he was genuinely concerned. What was the horse doing loose? What had happened to Josie? He vowed that if he found any harm had come to her, his first targets for revenge would be the three riders he had come across.

He climbed back into leather and started down the stream, leading the stray horse behind him. When he came to the point where the brook debouched into the main stream the Appaloosa he was leading began to pull at the rein. Brewer looked about him. The horse was definitely agitated about something and its unease was communicated to the pinto. Brewer dismounted once more and turned towards the brook, splashing his way forward, leading the two horses and searching the trees closely with his eyes.

Something about one of them caught his attention. A couple of branches looked to be damaged. He stepped up on the riverbank. A short way into the trees he came on an opening and saw a dark shape huddled on the grass. He knew it was Josie, knew that he had found her. With bated breath he rushed forward and, kneeling beside her, turned her face and put his ear to her lips. She was breathing clearly and in a few moments her eyes opened.

'Brewer!' she gasped.

He began to say something but the next moment all talk was suspended as he held her tight while she clung to him and they kissed. When they eventually broke away from one another Brewer propped her up against the tree. For a moment she winced as he did so.

'Are you OK?' he said, suddenly feeling embarrassed that he had not asked previously.

'I think so. The only real damage is to my ankle. I can't walk on it.'

'Should I take a look?'

'It might be better to leave it for the moment. It could be awkward taking off my boot.'

'Yeah.' Brewer looked up at the sky. 'You must be cold,' he said. 'It's too late to do anythin' much now so I'll build a fire and we'll make ourselves as comfortable as we can for the night. I'll rustle us up somethin' to eat as well.'

There were plenty of materials to hand so Brewer soon had a fire going. He got an old pan out of his warbag and a kettle which he filled with water from the brook. He put bacon and beans in the pan. When they had finished eating and were drinking black coffee, which Brewer had laced with a drop of whiskey, they were feeling quite comfortable and relaxed. It seemed natural for Josie to lie in his arms.

'I'm so glad you found me,' Josie said.

'Me too. I don't want to have to worry about you like that ever again.'

'You won't,' she replied.

She told him what had happened and

when she had finished Brewer looked grim.

'Once I get you back to the ranch,' he said, 'you'd better not move till this whole business has been concluded. I wouldn't put it past Sloane or any of his henchmen to try gettin' their hands on you. It might not have been planned this time, but you're not safe till Sloane has been dealt with.'

He didn't mention any of the conversation he had overheard from Josie's three stalkers, but he mentally made a note that he had one more score to settle with Choate.

The wheel of night rolled slowly overhead in the shape of a myriad revolving stars. Brewer grew calm once more and Josie was breathing peacefully. He thought she had fallen asleep but presently she shifted slightly and looked up at him.

'You're sure about this?' she asked.

'About what?'

She shrugged. 'About being with me. About . . . '

She paused, seeking the right words, and Brewer leaned down and kissed her on her brow.

'I'm sure about the way I feel about you. I just could never have imagined you might feel the same way too.'

'You are silly,' she said. 'Surely you must have guessed?'

Brewer shook his head. 'Still can't quite believe it,' he said.

She laughed gently and snuggled into him again.

'You might be good with horses and cattle,' she said. 'But you've a lot to learn about a woman.'

'I'm sure willin' to try,' Brewer replied.

Silence descended until Brewer had a sudden thought.

'Hey, what about your father?' he said.

Josie laughed again. 'Don't worry about him. He knows exactly how things are. You realize how much he respects you?'

'I hope you're right,' Brewer said.

'Believe me, so far as my father is concerned, things have worked out just fine,' she replied.

Brewer leaned forward to throw some branches on the fire. The flames licked up and illuminated the little clearing.

'You know, I used to come here when I was a girl,' Josie said. 'It was my favourite spot to get away and be by myself. I used to sit by the brook and read or sometimes I'd draw or write things in my diary. It was a special place. Now it's more special than ever.'

'Funny how things work out,' Brewer replied lamely.

'I remember when you first came. How old were you?'

'Thirteen,' Brewer replied.

'You were just a boy but I liked you from the start. There was always something kind of mysterious about how you arrived from nowhere. I guess I was intrigued.'

'I never knew my father. After my mother died I was brung up by a succession of strangers. One day I just lit out, stepped on a train and came West. Then Mr Hethridge took me on.'

'It must have been hard for you,' she said.

'Well, it's all changed now,' he replied.

★ ★ ★

The next morning Brewer was up early. From what he had gleaned from the conversation he had heard the night before, he had few fears that the Buzzard riders would come looking for Josie. It seemed they were under orders to wait for any passing stagecoach. It wasn't far back to the ranch but all the same, it made sense for them to be on their way. Josie's ankle was still a problem. He supported her while she hobbled to her horse and helped her into the saddle.

'Are you sure you can ride?' he said.

She smiled, although there was pain written across her features.

'Yes. I'll be fine.'

They splashed their way through the water, then rode up through the trees. As they were about to emerge on to the open range Brewer held up his hand as a signal for them to stop. Josie looked anxiously at him and he put his finger to his lips. Presently she heard what Brewer had heard, the sound of a horse's hoofs in the distance. Brewer reached behind his saddle-bags and brought out his field glasses. He put them to his eyes and picked out a horseman riding hard in the direction of the Buzzard On A Rail. The distance was too great for him to be able to pick out details, but he had a feeling it was Marshal Burke. He put the glasses back and looked at Josie.

'Coulda been the marshal. Nothin' to worry about,' he said.

Josie looked concerned. 'You're forgetting that as far as the marshal is concerned, you're still a wanted outlaw.'

'I wonder how far the marshal is involved with Sloane?' Brewer mused. 'Or is he his own man?' He was thinking that a time might soon come when the question would have to be answered.

Without further delay they came out of cover and set off in the direction of the Lone Pine at a steady trot. They were still quite a distance from the ranch house when the door was flung open and Hethridge came running down the steps to greet them. A second later the figure of Whipcrack Riley appeared on the veranda. Even from a distance Brewer could see the grin on the oldster's face. What had the old buzzard been up to? He would soon find out.

★　★　★

When the lawyer, Everard Hite, left his house to walk the short distance into town he had the distinct impression he was being followed. He glanced behind him several times without seeing anything but when he had reached his office he looked out of the window. He saw someone leaning against a post on the opposite side of the street who looked up at him.

Hite quickly withdrew and sat down at his desk. Since his meeting with Sloane he had been thinking about what the rancher had said and the more he thought about it the less he liked the situation. Sloane was not the kind of man to cross. So far he had kept well in with the big rancher, and the false documents assigning Sloane the rights to the Lone Pine were almost ready. Hite should have been content with that but instead, as he, Hite, now feared, he had overplayed his hand. It hadn't been wise to raise the question of how Sloane had come into possession of the Buzzard On A Rail. He had been a fool to think he could blackmail Sloane into giving him more money than he was likely to get by playing along with him with the false documents. He got to his feet and peered from behind the curtains once more. The man had not moved from the other side of the street and Hite was certain he was one of Sloane's men. What was he to do now?

He began to pace up and down the office wondering what his next step should be. His inclination was to cut his losses and get out altogether. Despite the work he had done on Sloane's behalf, he felt that things could never be the same again between them. Sloane was probably just waiting till he got his hands on the fake documents before dealing with the lawyer.

Maybe he should just get out of Eagle Creek and begin elsewhere? There was a lot to give up, though. Besides, it just wasn't safe to ride the stage at present. The coaches were not even running and it was doubtful whether the stage line would resume in the near future.

His thoughts turned to Marshal Burke. Maybe he should seek the protection of the law for what he feared Sloane might now do to him. He didn't have to say anything about his business with Sloane. At least he didn't need to admit to having forged any documents. But Burke was young and untried.

Worse still, he didn't seem the type to stand up to Sloane. If anything, he could be in Sloane's pocket. It was a tricky situation.

* * *

If he had gone to see the marshal, Hite would have found him quite amenable. The marshal at Rock Corner had been in touch with him about the stagecoach shootings and had sown a few seeds of doubt in Burke's mind concerning Sloane and his outfit. Up till now he had tended to take Sloane's side in several disputes, particularly where it concerned Hethridge and the Lone Pine.

Take the matter of the attempted hanging of Ben Brewer. Horse theft was a serious affair. Maybe Sloane had gone a bit too far in taking the matter into his own hands, but the fact of the crime remained. Nonetheless he was beginning to feel a little uneasy. Maybe he should have done more to check out the story. Maybe he should have looked into the question of whether the horse in question had carried the Buzzard On A Rail brand as Sloane had claimed.

That was one reason why he had set off early that morning to pay a visit to Sloane just to check out a few details. He had not been in the job very long since taking over on the retirement of the previous incumbent; he was finding there was more involved in being the representative of the law in Eagle Creek than he had bargained for.

★ ★ ★

Things had settled down at the Lone Pine following Brewer's arrival with Josie. After all the explanations had been made and they had all eaten, that young lady retired to her room, grateful to be able to rest her ankle and begin to recuperate from her experiences. Hethridge, Brewer and Riley had taken to the veranda to have a drink. It was mid-afternoon. The talk was desultory, each man sunk in his own thoughts while the main questions to be raised remained unspoken. Eventually Hethridge turned to Brewer.

'I haven't had a chance to say how grateful I am that you found Josie. I owe you.'

Brewer shuffled uncomfortably in his chair.

'You don't owe me nothin', Mr Hethridge,' he said. 'It's me that owes you.'

'Well, be that as it may, I'm glad that you and Josie seem to have admitted to your feelings at last.'

Brewer was even more uncomfortable and felt a warm flush rise to his cheeks.

'It's OK,' Hethridge said. 'It's been pretty obvious for some time the way you two young folks feel about one another. Like I say, I'm just glad it's all out in the open.'

'Of course, I — ' Brewer had begun, when Hethridge interrupted him.

'Don't say anything further. You don't have to justify yourself. As far as

I'm concerned, I couldn't have wished for a better outcome.'

Riley glanced across at the youngster. 'You're a lucky fella,' he remarked.

Nobody spoke for a few minutes. Looking out towards the river, Riley was the first to spot a rider coming towards them from that direction. He drew the attention of the others to the mounted figure.

'Ain't that Curly Evans?' he said.

Hethridge squinted. 'Yeah. And he seems to be a little agitated.'

They watched as Evans approached and slid from the saddle.

'Mr Hethridge,' he said, taking off his hat and holding it in his right hand, 'I'm sorry to disturb you but we seem to have some sort of problem down by the river.'

'Problem? What problem?'

'I don't rightly know how to put it. Fact is, the river's run dry.'

Hethridge gave Curly a puzzled look.

'The river's run dry? What do you mean?'

'Well, I was repairin' some fences down on the long range, just near the river. I guess I kinda noticed that it wasn't runnin' as freely as usual but when I took my hoss for a drink there was nothin' much more than a trickle.'

Hethridge looked at the others.

'How do you mean, a trickle? In all the time I've been here that stream has never run dry, not even in the worst drought. It's probably been that way for ever.'

'Well, it ain't now. Like I say, when I looked there weren't hardly enough water to dampen the soil. I got straight on my horse and come back to tell you.'

'I appreciate it,' Hethridge said. He jumped to his feet. 'Stay here and keep an eye on Miss Josie,' he said to Curly. 'Help yourself to a drink.'

He turned to Brewer and Riley: 'Come on,' he added. 'Let's take a look.'

When they got down to the Deep Fork they found it just as Curly had said. In the middle of the channel a thin trickle of water was all that was left of the normally flowing stream. The exposed mud gave off a foul smell and black flies hovered over it. Hethridge looked up and down the riverbank.

'I don't understand,' he said.

Brewer looked worried. 'It's lucky we got those beeves on the hoof,' he remarked. 'But I don't see how we'll be able to manage for long without a water supply.'

Riley looked hard at them both. 'You know what's happened?' he said.

They turned their faces to him.

'This is all part of Sloane's campaign to get you to sell up,' Riley said. 'It's no accident. What he's done is dam up the stream deliberately to deprive you of water. I've seen it happen before.'

Hethridge thought for a moment.

'Hell, Riley's right,' he exclaimed. 'That varmint has got to be behind it.' He spat into the thin thread of water that trickled through the mud. 'This time he's gone too far,' he said grimly. 'This time he's goin' to pay.'

He wheeled his horse about.

'Come on,' he cried. 'What are we waitin' for?'

Brewer looked at Riley.

'Come on,' Hethridge repeated. 'Let's get ridin'.'

'What you got in mind, Mr Hethridge?' Riley said.

'What the hell else would I have in mind other than gettin' over to the Buzzard and pronto.'

'What about Miss Josie?' Riley said.

Hethridge's mouth opened and then closed again.

'If you don't mind me sayin' so,' Riley continued, 'this situation is somethin' that needs thinkin' about.' Seeing that Hethridge was about to expostulate, he continued: 'We're all agreed Sloane has gone too far this time. He needs to be dealt with. But we don't want to go off at half cock. Let's just take a bit of time to think this through.'

Even without Riley's reminder, Brewer was thinking of Josie.

'Riley's right,' he said. 'I think we

should go back to the ranch and work things out.'

Hethridge had calmed down a little. He was seeing the sense in what the two men were telling him, although he was still fighting his urge to go straight ahead and act immediately. He looked up and down the river once more.

'OK,' he said. 'But this is war.'

Without pausing for a reply, he wheeled his horse and began to ride back towards the ranch house. Brewer and Riley exchanged glances; then, both of them grim-faced, they rode after him.

*　*　*

Marshal Burke's visit to the Buzzard On A Rail had given him something to think about, and he hadn't been back in Eagle Creek for long when he was surprised to receive a visit from Everard Hite. In the course of his job he had had some dealings with the lawyer, and he did not like him. He ushered Hite to a seat, then looked at him with a stony face, waiting for the lawyer to open the conversation.

'Marshal Burke,' Hite began, 'I'm here because I have reason to believe my life may be under threat.' He paused but the marshal remained silent. 'If you don't mind, would you just come to the window for a moment?'

Burke got to his feet and followed Hite to where he stood peering cautiously into the street.

'There!' Hite said.

'What am I lookin' for?'

'Across the street. A mean-looking man with a red shirt and black waistcoat.'

Burke twitched the curtain and glanced out. He recognized the man Hite was pointing out as one of Sloane's Buzzard On A Rail hands.

'What about him?'

'He keeps watching and following me. I need protection. I need you to say something to him.'

Burke returned to his desk, followed a moment after by the lawyer. Burke looked at him. If Hite had been somewhat agitated when he came in, he was clearly in some distress now.

'Perhaps you'd better tell me what this is all about,' Burke said.

★ ★ ★

Back at the Lone Pine a serious discussion was taking place between Hethridge, Brewer and Riley. Curly Evans had been invited to join them. Hethridge's anger at finding the Deep Fork dammed had subsided and been replaced by a steely determination.

'OK,' he said. 'Let's see what we got. It's pretty obvious that all the incidents that have been taking place recently are down to Sloane and the Buzzard On A Rail. From what Riley has told us we now know what the reason is. He wants to get his hands on the Lone Pine in order to sell off the rights of way across the range to the Plains and Western Railroad Company. Between them, by the way, they've also been leanin' on Drewitt and his stagecoach line.' He paused to take a drink of coffee.

'Just lately, startin' with the attempted lynchin' of Brewer here, things have got a lot worse. Now Sloane's dammed up the river. Unless we do somethin', we might as well just give the ranch away.'

'Why don't we take it to Marshal Burke?' Curly said. 'Let the law sort it out.'

'That's a problem, as I see it,' Hethridge said. 'I would agree with you if the marshal was someone we could trust. Trouble is, he's weak and more inclined to listen to Sloane than do anythin' that might upset the apple cart.'

'Then we got to take the law into our own hands,' Brewer said.

Riley had remained quiet during this exchange. Now he spoke.

'Seems to me,' he said, 'that we're maybe underestimating the marshal. He needs to be convinced that Sloane is the problem here. Sooner or later the law is goin' to have to be involved.'

'Already is,' Brewer interjected. 'Have you forgotten we're both still wanted men?'

'I wouldn't put too much stress on that,' Riley said. 'Fact is, I've had a few words with Burke. He ain't exactly convinced of our innocence, but I think he might be more open-minded than we've given him credit for. At least, if it could be demonstrated to him that Sloane is responsible for all the trouble.'

'I see your point,' Hethridge said, 'but you're not makin' a lot of sense otherwise. Sure, it would be nice if the marshal could be made to see what's really goin' on, but how do you propose to do it?'

'By showin' him that Sloane's behind the attacks on the railroad company.'

Hethridge laughed. 'Yeah, that would do the trick,' he said. 'Trouble is, apart from anythin' else, the stage ain't even runnin' just at the moment.'

'Yes it is,' Riley said. 'In fact the run between Eagle Creek and Lansberg is scheduled for tomorrow.'

The other three looked at him questioningly.

'Drewitt can't get anybody to drive

the stage or ride shotgun. And no passengers are goin' to be willin' to take the risk of bein' killed,' Hethridge said.

'There won't be any passengers, leastways not regular ones,' Riley said. 'And I'll be drivin' it.'

There was a moment's silence. The others exchanged glances. A slow grin had spread across Riley's countenance at the sight of their evident consternation.

'I think I'd better explain,' he said. 'When I left you yesterday I went to see Jim Drewitt. I know him pretty well. Like I told young Brewer here, I used to ride for the Eagle Creek line. The upshot of it was that I've arranged to take out the stage tomorrow.

'My original idea was just to show folks that the stagecoach is still a goin' concern. I also figured to maybe flush out whoever was behind the attacks on the stage. Then I figured that it might also be an opportunity to show Marshal Burke who was behind it, if he could be persuaded to ride along.

'Of course, I'd be takin' a chance that the stage might not be attacked this time, but I've took a few steps to spread the word that it'll be carryin' some gold bullion. That might help draw down the Buzzard gunnies.

'But things are even better. Thanks to Brewer, we now know where the attack is likely to take place. The whole thing is beginnin' to work out even better than I hoped.'

'You mean you've already spoken to the marshal? Hell, you were takin' a chance, weren't you?' Hethridge exclaimed. 'You could have ended up in jail.'

Riley shrugged. 'Maybe so,' he replied, 'but I reckon I've been around long enough to be able to make a pretty fair judgement about a man.'

'You didn't have much to go on.'

'The marshal's a young fella. He's just learnin'.'

It was Hethridge's turn to grin. 'Yeah, and I guess you did a good job of helpin' him come round to your point of view.'

Riley poured more coffee for himself and the others. There was silence while they assimilated what he had told them.

'Seems a lot is hangin' on that young whipper-snapper Burke,' Hethridge said.

'He's the law. The best way is to let the law deal with Sloane.'

Hethridge nodded.

'I've seen what happens when a range war gets started,' Riley mused. 'A lot of people tend to die and nothin' gets settled.'

Brewer glanced at him, wondering what experience the oldster had on which to base his conclusions. Riley looked from one to the other of the group.

'I got me a passenger,' he said. 'I could still be doin' with someone to ride shotgun.'

★ ★ ★

Early next morning those citizens of Eagle Creek who were astir were surprised to see the stagecoach standing outside the depot with a team of horses being fastened to the traces. Drewitt had polished the Concord up so that it looked at its brightest and best. The scarlet paintwork gleamed and the yellow wheels showed not a trace of dust or dirt.

Standing alongside were Brewer and Curly, while, having clambered on top, Whipcrack Riley was making some adjustments to the roof rack.

When he was satisfied with the arrangements for the baggage Riley climbed down and went inside the depot. A few minutes later he emerged carrying the most extravagant looking whip that either Brewer or Curly had ever clapped eyes on.

'It's my own,' Whipcrack said. 'You might say Drewitt's been keepin' it in storage.'

Brewer held out his hand. 'Let me take a closer look,' he said.

The whip was a beauty. It had a buckskin lash over twenty feet in length, about twice as long as a normal whip. This was attached to a shaft some five feet long, made of stout hickory ornamented with handcrafted silver designs. The lash was oiled and pliable as a snake.

'Just hold on to that thing for a moment,' Riley said.

He disappeared inside the depot again. This time he was gone for slightly longer but when he emerged once more his appearance had changed. Over his normal worn and serviceable attire he had thrown a long yellow linen duster. His arms were encased in leather gauntlets, he wore tall leather boots and his white locks flowed out beneath a wide-brimmed felt hat with a low crown. Brewer handed him the whip.

'You sure look the part,' he said.

Curly grinned. 'Brewer's feelin' a whole lot safer already. That outfit is gonna dazzle any marksman.'

Riley gave a wry smile. 'Any sign of the marshal?' he said.

Brewer looked down the street. The figure of the marshal had just hove into view.

'Comin' right now,' he replied. 'I was beginnin' to get a bit worried. This whole scheme of yours would look a little cockamamie if he changed his mind.'

'You mean it don't already?' Curly cracked.

The marshal was carrying an iron-framed Winchester rifle and wore his two guns slung low.

'That's a good sign he's expectin' somethin' to happen,' Brewer remarked.

The marshal acknowledged the waiting group with a nod.

'All right,' Riley called. 'Everybody ready? Then let's get rollin'.'

The marshal and Curly took their seats inside the stagecoach while Riley and Brewer swung themselves up top. Brewer cradled his sawed down shotgun across his chest.

'Maybe you better just put that aside for the moment,' Riley said. 'We got a good run from here to Rock Corner and then another section to Lansberg. If what you overheard is correct, those varmints aren't likely to strike till we hit that last section.'

'That's where they were hidin' out. Ain't to say Sloane hasn't got another little surprise planned for us some-wheres along the route.'

'Well, wherever they hit, we'll be ready for 'em. I reckon that between us we got more artillery than Ulysses S Grant.'

Riley took a final look round. He took the reins in his hand, then his whip licked out with a sharp crack.

'Don't like to do that normally,' he said. 'Scares the passengers.'

With a lurch the stagecoach rumbled forward. A few people strolling along the boardwalks stopped to admire the passing show and a dog ran across the street in front of the horses.

'By the way,' Brewer said, 'what happened to Drewitt? I figured he'd be there to see us off.'

'He's got business in Rock Corner. We'll see him there.'

★ ★ ★

Soon the coach was rattling along at a decent speed and the main street of Eagle Creek was left behind. The Concord rocked from side to side and already Brewer was finding it more than a little uncomfortable, but Riley seemed to be in his element. As the coach rattled along he leaned out to spit occasionally and, with his knee raised to support his arm, he appeared to be enjoying himself. Clouds of dust hung in the air behind them and rose to Brewer's throat. He coughed as he peered through the haze.

'You'll soon get used to it,' Riley shouted. 'In the meantime, use your bandanna if you have to.'

'What happens when things get really dusty?' Brewer said. 'It must have got bad on that old San Antonio run you were tellin' me about.'

'Yeah. Sometimes it got so that you couldn't see anythin' in front of you.'

Brewer thought that one over. 'So how could you tell where you were goin'?' he asked.

'Sometimes by the sound of the wheels, sometimes by smell. If things got real bad we just whipped up the hosses and let them do the thinkin'.'

Brewer peered at the oldster. There was a grin on his face and Brewer wasn't sure whether to take him seriously.

'I thought you said they used mules?'

'Mules, hosses, makes no difference. We still got there.'

The coach rumbled on. They were cutting across a corner of Lone Pine range and Brewer guessed they must be somewhere near where the Plains and Western planned to build their railroad link.

'I hope this works out,' Brewer said. 'If those Buzzard varmints don't attack, we're gonna be lookin' pretty silly.'

'Likely to look it anyway,' Riley said. 'And the way Burke's carryin' all that artillery, I reckon he's more than ready to march us straight to the jailhouse if he hasn't got anyone else. Might do it whatever happens.'

Brewer thought for a moment. 'Kind

of strange, isn't it?' he said. 'I mean, ridin' along like this and hopin' to get attacked. Kind of tips things upside down, if you see what I mean.'

Riley nodded. 'Yeah, guess so.' He turned his head. 'How do you feel about bein' the number one target? By all accounts, whoever killed those other messengers is a pretty good shot.'

Brewer shifted uneasily in his seat. 'Hadn't looked at it that way,' he said.

'Well,' Riley said, 'we'll just have to see what happens.'

The next couple of hours passed by uneventfully, then a few straggling shacks indicated that they were approaching Rock Corner.

'We'll make a stop here,' Riley said. 'Drewitt should be waitin' for us to arrive.'

'Are we pickin' him up?' Brewer asked.

'Nope.' Riley gave Brewer an amused look. 'There will be one passenger, but it ain't Drewitt.'

Brewer was puzzled. 'Who else would it be if it's not Drewitt?' he asked. They were rattling down the main drag of Rock Corner.

'Wait a few minutes and you'll see,' Riley replied.

The stage depot came into view and with a tug of the reins Riley brought the four horses to a halt. Before he or Brewer could step down the stage doors opened and the marshal got out, followed by Curly. The marshal looked up at Riley.

'I hope you're not wastin' my time,' he said.

Riley did not reply because just at that moment Drewitt appeared in the doorway of the depot.

'Howdy!' he shouted. 'Good to see you, Riley!'

'Good to see you,' Riley replied. He climbed down from his seat.

'So far, so good,' Drewitt said.

'In a way,' Riley replied. 'But remember, we're hopin' to flush out those varmints who attacked the stage the last couple of times.'

Drewitt's face was rueful. 'Yes, of

course. I kinda forgot. It's just seein' the old stage back on the road . . . '

'What about our extra passenger?' Riley said.

Drewitt's expression changed in an instant. 'Right in here.'

He made to go into the depot but then turned back again. 'No, you wait here. I'll go fetch him.'

Brewer was still sitting on top of the coach. He watched the retreating figure of Drewitt, not knowing what to expect. In a few moments the stage owner returned leading a figure by the arm. There were a few people standing in the doorway and Brewer couldn't make things out clearly. Whoever the figure was, Brewer didn't recognize him. He seemed strangely inert, then Brewer heard Riley laugh. Looking closer, he realized the figure was a dummy.

'Come on!' Riley shouted. 'Give me and Drewitt a hand to pass him up.'

Without quite realizing what was going on, Brewer reached down and took hold of the dummy as it was handed up to him. In another moment he had fastened it so it was beside him atop the coach.

'You can get down now,' Riley laughed. 'Looks like your spell as shotgun messenger is finished. We got another guard now.'

Brewer propped the dummy up straighter and then climbed down. 'OK, Riley,' he said. 'Just what's goin' on?'

Curly and the marshal were standing open-mouthed, waiting for an explanation.

'Isn't it obvious?' Riley said. 'Me and Drewitt came up with the idea. We know that whoever shot those two guards is very good with a rifle. One bullet was enough to take out the last man. So why put anyone at an unnecessary risk? From a distance nobody is goin' to be able to tell whether it's a real man sittin' on the roof of the stage or a dummy. The shootist certainly won't be expectin' a dummy. So when he takes a shot, it's the dummy who'll take the hit. And we'll have a good idea just where the varmint is hidin'.'

Curly broke into a laugh. The

marshal looked unconvinced.

'It's a clever idea,' Drewitt said. 'Leastways, we thought so.'

Riley turned to Brewer. 'So you see, you don't have to worry. From this point on you take your seat in the stage along with Curly and the marshal. Enjoy the ride!'

Brewer pursed his mouth. 'You'll still be up there,' he pointed out. 'With any luck the gunman will go for the driver this time.'

Riley laughed again. 'No need to take it like that,' he joked. 'Come on, you got to admit it's a good idea. And it'll work.'

Brewer grinned. 'Should make a good companion for you,' he quipped. 'As if one dummy weren't enough!'

The marshal didn't seem at all amused. 'I hope this whole thing ain't some kind of a joke,' he commented.

'No joke,' Drewitt said. 'Two men been killed ridin' shotgun. Nope, it ain't no joke.'

'Then let's get rollin'.'

Following his words, the marshal

opened the door and stepped inside the stagecoach. Curly followed, then Brewer rather reluctantly took his seat.

'Sure you don't want to take a ride?' Riley said to Drewitt.

The stage owner hesitated. He hadn't been intending to join the stage but something was urging him to do so. He turned on his heel and went through the door of the depot. In a few moments he reappeared carrying a Sharps .50 rifle.

'Don't expect to see no buffalo,' Riley remarked.

'She's sighted for dry-gulchers,' Drewitt replied.

He stepped into the coach. Riley climbed up and took his place on the driver's seat.

'Regular war wagon I'm drivin',' he said.

There was no reply.

'Better keep a close lookout from now on,' he continued.

When there was no answer he turned, then broke into a laugh. He had forgotten that Brewer had been replaced by the dummy. It held a mock-up shotgun across its chest. From close range it looked less than convincing.

Riley raised his arm and his long whip cracked. The horses took the load and the stagecoach moved forward, lurching down the main street of Rock Corner, which was soon left behind. Riley turned to the dummy again. Brewer had made a decent effort at fastening it down but it had slipped slightly. He reached across and propped it up, feeling suddenly exposed. His eyes searched the landscape, then concentrated on looking ahead, seeking for any sign of trouble.

Inside the coach the four passengers had taken up positions at the windows and were also on the alert, their weapons held in readiness. Brewer was searching for any landmarks he might recognize but he could see nothing distinctive. For the first time he began to have real doubts about Riley's plan. The further they got towards Lansberg the less likely was the possibility of an attack. Again he was struck by the oddness of the situation, that instead of a clear and safe run they were hoping to draw down an assault.

He glanced at the marshal. Burke had his rifle across his lap but for the moment he had turned away from the window. It was obvious that he was thinking the whole exercise was turning out to be a waste of time. Brewer turned back. As the landscape raced past he found his thoughts turning to Josie. He was a fortunate man. He could still hardly believe the way things had turned out.

Just then the trail took a bend and the coach swayed. They were being bumped and jolted all the way. Brewer was glad that Lansberg was the last stop on this particular journey. He wouldn't have relished carrying on beyond that point. But before they got to Lansberg there was the little matter of who was behind the stagecoach attacks to be resolved for the marshal's benefit, and if it was to be settled it had to be soon.

6

Before anything actually happened, Riley knew it was coming. From the high point of a ridge he caught a glint and he knew it was sunlight reflecting from the barrel of a gun. The next moment there was a crump of air and a booming reverberation. The dummy jumped and then slipped sideways. Although there was no need, Riley called to the others, then instinctively he cracked his whip and the horses burst forward, redoubling their pace so that the stagecoach fairly flew along the dusty track.

At the same moment a bunch of horsemen broke from cover and began to ride down on the stagecoach. Despite his desperate position, Riley couldn't suppress a grin. The plan was working out. Attracted by the lure of easy pickings, the bushwhackers were ignoring their previous practice and attacking the coach openly, not knowing that inside was a group of well-armed men.

Brewer, positioned on the side of the coach facing the rising ground from which the attackers were coming, counted six of them, so the ones he had come across had obviously been joined by others. They were getting closer but the coach was still tearing along the trail and Brewer was beginning to wonder whether Riley had forgotten the next part of the plan in the fury of the moment. The marshal and Drewitt had their rifles raised and Curly was already about to let loose.

'Not yet!' Brewer shouted.

So far they had acted exactly as a stagecoach under assault would do, but the next moment the coach lurched and suddenly began to slow. Dust rose in dense clouds as Riley hauled on the brake, then the coach slid to a shuddering halt, swinging round and swerving partly off the trail. For a few moments Brewer's vision was obscured not only by dust but by the new angle at which the coach had slurred to a stop, but in a moment he had sighted a couple of the riders who were now bearing down fast on the stationary Concord. He glanced quickly at the others.

'OK,' he shouted. 'Let 'em have it.'

At his words a tremendous burst of fire broke out from inside the coach. The bushwhackers, all unsuspecting, were hit by a hail of lead. Up top, Riley, lying prone on the roof, opened fire with his shotgun. Two of the riders on Brewer's side flung up their arms and toppled from their horses. A third rider came into view just as his horse went down, throwing him from the saddle. There came a lull and then some further sporadic shots.

Brewer opened the door of the coach and, keeping close to the side, moved forward to investigate. Two of the riders had turned and were heading back up the slope from which they had come down. The other four lay sprawled in various positions in the grass alongside three of the horses. Other bodies of men and horses lay on the opposite side of the coach.

One horse was standing at a little distance and as Brewer looked the man who had fallen from it suddenly appeared from behind some rocks, running hard in an effort to reach it. A shot rang out from Drewitt's side of the coach but the man was more or less out of range. He sprang into the saddle and wheeled away, shouting something as he did so. Brewer couldn't quite catch the words and then they were lost on the wind as the rider spurred his horse away.

Just then there was a sound behind him and Brewer spun, his finger on the trigger of his shotgun. Even as he did so he realized he was too late. The man he was facing had the drop on him and his finger was already closing on the trigger when there came a loud crack like a clap of thunder and the man staggered back, dropping his rifle and clutching at his throat. Brewer didn't know what had happened till he saw the lash of Riley's whip tightening around the gunny's neck. The man's face was purple and he was making strained gurgling sounds. His feet came off the ground and then he fell like a spilt sack of grain as Riley released him. Brewer glanced up as the grizzled face of the oldster appeared over the rim of the coach.

'You've got somethin' to learn yet,' Riley cracked. 'That was a mighty close call.'

He climbed down and they were joined by the others. The marshal began to walk away towards one of the fallen horses. They watched him bend down and examine the carcass. He stood erect and called out.

'Buzzard On A Rail. Looks like you were right.' He came back to join them.

'The plan worked,' Drewitt said. 'What now?'

'Reckon I need to get on and pay a

visit to Jed Sloane,' the marshal said.

Riley was looking thoughtful. 'The one that got away,' he said. 'He shouted somethin'.'

'Yeah. I couldn't make it out, though,' Brewer replied.

'Just cursin', I should think,' Curly remarked. 'Guess he had good cause.'

'I thought I heard mention of the name of the Lone Pine,' Riley said.

'Cursin' that as well,' Drewitt replied.

'He had no reason to associate what happened here with the Lone Pine,' Riley said.

'Maybe he recognized you or Brewer or Curly?'

'Maybe, but it don't seem likely.'

Riley looked down at the limp shape of the man he had lassoed with his whip. He was still breathing.

'I got a feelin',' Riley said, 'that maybe that shout wasn't meant for us but for him.'

Brewer was suddenly concerned. 'You mean, maybe he was tellin' him to meet at the Lone Pine?'

His brow was wrinkled in concentration. 'But that don't make sense.'

'It would make sense if they was plannin' some sort of attack on the Lone Pine.'

'Goldurn it, if you're right they could have done so already.'

The five of them looked at each other.

'Only one way to find out, and that's get there as quick as we can,' said Riley.

Brewer looked down at the injured man. 'What about him?' he said.

'He can take his chances. Right now we ain't got time to lose.'

'We ain't got our regular hosses,' the marshal said.

'We got the stage. Come on. Let's get movin'!'

The marshal, Drewitt and Curly piled inside while Brewer rejoined Riley on the roof of the coach.

'Better hold on to your hat,' Riley said. 'This is goin' to be one hell of a ride!'

He took the reins in his hand and,

calling to the frightened horses he manoeuvred the stage so that it was facing the way they had come. Then his whip cracked once more and they were rattling down the trail. They hadn't gone far when he turned to Brewer.

'You know this territory better than me,' he shouted. 'There's gotta be a better way than goin' all the way back through Eagle Creek.'

'Yeah, I guess you're right.'

'You work out what's the quickest route. I guess it must be somewhere over thataway.'

Brewer pointed to his left. The country looked pretty rough and broken. A little way beyond Lansberg they would have been on the edge of the badlands. This was bad enough.

'You ain't figurin' to head there?' Riley shouted. 'Hell, there's no sort of trail that I can see.'

'Never mind that,' Brewer said. 'Just keep your fingers crossed these hosses are up to it.'

Riley thought hard. They were

travelling back towards Rock Creek in a roughly easterly direction. The Lone Pine was generally north and west.

'That way!' he shouted, pointing in a direction similar to that which Brewer had indicated.

Riley carried on for about another quarter of a mile and then, pulling hard on the reins, he turned the stagecoach off the trail. The Concord shook from side to side but soon they were picking up the pace again. There was a shout from inside the coach.

'Better let them know what's happenin',' Riley said.

Brewer looked at the oldster, then, adjusting his foothold, leaned over the side of the coach so his head was almost level with the open window.

'What the hell is Riley doin'?' It was the voice of Drewitt.

'Just makin' a little detour!' Brewer called. 'Save time!'

'Tell the old buzzard he's out of a job if there's any damage to the stage!'

Brewer swung himself erect again.

Just then the coach hit a depression in the ground and he was almost flung off. His stomach lurched and then he was bouncing hard on the seat as the Concord rattled up the opposite slope.

'Missed that one!' Riley grinned. 'Expect there'll be plenty more before I get my eye in.'

As far as Brewer could tell the oldster was just aiming the coach blind. In fact he was looking out for any slight vestige of a track, which might ease the dangers and discomfort of the ride. There were faint trails across the prairie which had been made by riders passing through or antelope looking for water. A broader stretch of trampled grass indicated the passage of buffalo and Riley held to that track as long as it stretched in the general direction he wished to go. But there was not much else that he could do.

Soon Brewer was feeling sore with the constant bumping and shaking. He didn't know whether it was any less uncomfortable inside the coach but at least there would be little danger of being thrown off altogether. Still, the very process of trying to remain on the roof of the stagecoach helped to distract his mind from the worrying thought of what might be happening back at the Lone Pine, and in particular to Josie. Or maybe they were off on a wild-goose chase. They had only the gunman's shouted words to go by. Well, if they were wrong, it wouldn't matter. The marshal had had his proof and that was the point of the exercise.

They had been travelling for a considerable period of time, although Brewer for one seemed to have lost all sense of it, and there was beginning to be something more familiar about the landscape. When Brewer saw a line of trees in the distance he knew they were not far from where he had ridden down the brook.

He shouted to Riley, drawing his attention to the trees and indicating that he should veer slightly and follow a course parallel to them. Riley's whip

cracked and the horses turned, straining hard, foam now flying from their
mouths. Whether they could scent the
presence of water or whether it was for
some other reason, they seemed to step
out with a fresh influx of vigour. Riley
let them have their heads but he was no
fool. He knew how to pace them and
after a spell of fast going he eased them
down.

'They're a good team,' Riley shouted.
'I guess Drewitt had a point to make.'

The coach had been spick and span
when it set off from Eagle Creek. Now
it was unrecognizable as the same
vehicle, being crusted with dust and
mire. It had taken even more of a
battering after Riley turned off the trail,
and it seemed a wonder to Brewer that
it held together at all. They had set off
quite early and now the sun was already
well down the western sky. The terrain
was becoming increasingly familiar to
Brewer and he knew they didn't have
too far to go. Suddenly he tensed.
Ahead of them he could discern a faint

smudge on the skyline and he drew Riley's attention to it.

'Could be a dust devil,' Riley replied.

'It's smoke,' Brewer said.

Riley made no further comment. Brewer turned his head to look at him; he could see that the oldster's mouth was set in a grim line. Riley raised his whip and cracked it over the heads of the horses. After the comparative rest they had been enjoying they were reinvigorated and broke into a fresh trot which, under Riley's urging, soon grew into as regular a gallop as they were capable of while dragging the weight of the Concord behind them.

The thin plume of smoke ascended higher. There was a knocking on the roof of the stagecoach and a shout which indicated that the others had seen it too. Brewer realized that it could only mean one thing. The Lone Pine ranch, or part of it, had been set alight. Sloane must have finally lost patience. Brewer wished they had left more men to defend it but a lot of the ranch hands were with the trail drive. His only consolation was that many of the Buzzard On A Rail's hands would be similarly engaged.

Now it seemed to Brewer that the stagecoach was going at a snail's pace and he urged Riley to greater speed. As they came nearer to the Lone Pine they could hear the sound of shooting. The coach was rattling and rolling its way up a slope and when they emerged on its crest they could see the ranch in front of them. Smoke was beginning to pour from one of the outhouses, but so far the main building appeared to be unaffected.

Brewer could see at a glance that the place was surrounded. He couldn't make out individual figures but it was clear just where most of them were placed. He was observing as much of the scene as he could. In the immediate foreground the land descended to the river which lay between the stagecoach and the ranch.

He was just wondering what Riley

intended to do next when the stage-coach, which had come almost to a halt at the crest of the rise, suddenly shot forward again and began the descent towards the river, soon picking up speed so that it was going at a breakneck pace.

'What the hell!' Brewer began but his words were obliterated in the rattle and thunder of the headlong rush towards the river. The ground flew past and the Concord rocked and swayed so much that it seemed it must overturn, but somehow it remained upright. Brewer was hanging on for dear life and expecting the worst when they hit the river. Then he remembered that it had been dammed and there was no water.

The horses clattered over the river-bank and the coach lurched forward, almost flinging Brewer from his perch. It righted itself and then bumped its way over the mud and stones of the riverbed. The little shallow pools of water that remained gleamed in the afternoon sunlight.

As the stage approached the middle point of the riverbed it slowed right down so that it seemed it must get stuck, but Riley, exercising all his skill, kept the horses moving forward. The opposite riverbank loomed but it shelved gently so that the horses were able to take it in their stride. The coach came up from what had been the Deep Fork with only its wheels dampened.

'What now?' Brewer yelled.

Riley grinned. 'Ain't no stoppin' her now,' he shouted. 'I told you she was a regular war wagon.'

Sloane's men had obviously taken notice of the stagecoach because some of the shooting was now aimed in its direction. Brewer raised his shotgun and began to blast away; a cannonade of gunfire from within the coach told him that the others had the same idea. Like some mad Jehu, Riley cracked his curling whip, urging the horses to one last lung-bursting effort. Now the coach was almost among the attackers and lead was being flung from the windows in a storm of death and destruction.

Some of Sloane's men were running in various directions, only to be cut down by the hail of bullets streaming from the gaudy chariot. Brewer's double-barrelled shotgun was spraying 00 buckshot like a spendthrift throwing coins and not much was being wasted. Fire was being returned but the speed of the coach rendered the shots ineffective.

Just ahead of them a figure appeared from behind a bush, but before the man could fire, Riley's whip curled out and the man staggered back, dropping his rifle and clutching at his cheek which had been ripped like paper from the brow to the chin.

The coach rattled on and it seemed that Riley had lost control as it burst into the yard outside the ranch house. He tugged on the reins and the coach swerved to one side, rounding the corner of the veranda and heading towards the barn, from which flames were now shooting through the roof.

Just ahead was a water trough and as the horses veered away to avoid it, the coach reared up on two wheels and then turned over with a tremendous crash. Brewer was hurled from his seat and landed heavily on the packed dirt of the yard. For a few moments he lay stunned, then, as his senses returned, he was relieved to see Riley on his knees crawling towards him while from the open door of the overturned coach the figures of the marshal, Curly and Drewitt were emerging. Plumes of dust rose from the earth around Riley and then, realizing his own exposed position, Brewer rolled to the shelter of the water trough as Riley came up alongside him, still holding his whip.

Brewer had lost his shotgun but he was soon blazing away with his Colts. He looked over to the barn where the others had taken up various positions. The crackling of the fire was loud and a dense cloud of smoke hung in the air above the barn. Riley had drawn his own six-guns and was firing very deliberately towards the front of the ranch house, where most of the shooting aimed at them was coming from. It seemed to Brewer that it had become more sporadic and he was feeling that they were getting the better of the struggle when he heard a scream which sent his blood cold.

'Josie!' he exclaimed.

Riley ducked as a bullet sent up a spray of water.

'That scream came from inside the house,' Brewer said. 'Whipcrack, keep me covered. I'm goin' to make a break.'

Riley nodded. Without a second thought Brewer was on his feet, doubled over, and running to the veranda, where he rounded the corner and made for the door. Shots were still coming from the windows and he ducked beneath them. Bullets thudded into the walls, sending splinters of wood flying into the air, and he felt a tug at his shoulder as a bullet caught at his jacket sleeve, narrowly missing shattering his already injured arm.

Now he was at the door, and without hesitation he hurled himself against it. It was unlocked and Brewer went crashing through to land unceremoniously on his backside. For a moment he had a glimpse of a rifle pointing at him, then he heard Hethridge's single exclamation of surprise.

'Brewer!'

Brewer didn't wait to acknowledge the ranch-owner or answer any questions. Instead he made for the stairs and raced up them two at a time. As he did so there was another scream and Brewer guessed it was from Josie's bedroom. He ran down the short corridor, found the door open and flung himself inside. A bullet whistled past his ear and ricocheted from something near by. He dived for the floor as another bullet thudded into the wood of the door, then he rolled over and rose quickly to his feet, his six-gun in his hand. Josie was standing by the window and immediately behind her, with one arm around her neck and his right hand holding a gun to her head, was Choate.

'One more move and the lady dies!' Choate hissed.

Josie was looking at Brewer with terror and a mute appeal in her eyes.

'Let her go,' Brewer said.

'Throw the gun aside,' Choate responded.

Brewer was weighing up his chances of getting in a killing shot but quickly rejected the idea. It was too dangerous. Choate drew back the hammer of his six-gun.

'Do it!' he snapped.

Brewer raised the weapon. 'Don't be stupid, Choate. Even if you fire you can't be sure I wouldn't get a shot off in return. It's a stalemate. Better cut your losses.'

Choate licked his lips.

'I'll make a deal,' Brewer continued. 'Just leave the girl and you can walk away.'

The sounds of shooting outside were dwindling away but the crackling of flames was loud and smoke was drifting in through the open window.

'I guess you came in that way,' Brewer said. 'You can either get out the same way or I will personally guarantee you a safe passage through the house. Just release the lady.'

Choate glanced towards the window. Then his dull, flat eyes swivelled back to Brewer. There was a slight twitch and as his hand moved Brewer knew he was about to fire. Brewer threw himself forward, pitching into the pair of them as the shot grazed his temple. All three went over as a second shot from Choate's gun buried itself in the ceiling.

Brewer's gun had flown from his grasp and he was concentrating on trying to protect Josie. Choate was back on his feet and his gun was pointed at Brewer but when he pulled the trigger there was a click as the hammer fell on an empty chamber. Choate hurled the gun at Brewer's head and made for the window.

Although the ranch house was built on two floors, the ceilings were low and it was not a big drop to the ground below. Choate jumped and began running hard towards the rear of the building, making for the trees where he had left his horse. There were still sounds of shooting coming from the front but things were quiet at the back and he hadn't far to go as he rounded the blazing barn. There was only a matter of yards to go when suddenly he felt a sudden sharp pain in his legs and his feet gave way beneath him. He thought he must have crashed into something on the ground and made to get back up but found he couldn't move. Something held his legs in a vice. Glancing down, he saw that they were lashed together, then he heard footsteps. He looked up to see the gnarled features of Whipcrack Riley outlined against the flames of the burning barn.

'You, old man!' Choate breathed.

'Remember me?' Riley said. 'Seems like you and me and ropes just kinda go together. Maybe you'll be havin' a date with another one.'

Back in the ranch house Brewer had led Josie down the stairs, where she collapsed into the grateful arms of her father. Brewer was about to take up a position at one of the windows when he was struck by a sudden thought. Was the pinto, Flume, in the blazing barn? Sometimes horses had been stabled there.

Quickly, Brewer made for the kitchen, looking for a back door. It was locked and he undid the bolt. He ran into the open, bent over to make himself as small a target as he could. A shot whistled by his head but he made it to the barn.

Covering his mouth with his bandanna for protection, he peered inside. He couldn't make much out at first through the smoke and he was soon forced to withdraw because of the searing heat, but he had seen enough to assure him that there were no horses. The barn was empty but for some piles of hay.

He turned away and, under cover of the far side of the burning barn, he made his way to the corrals. Most of the horses were with the remuda but there were no signs of any of the ones that had been left behind. Then he saw that a rail had been broken. The frightened horses must have bolted.

As if to confirm Brewer's thoughts there came a neighing sound from somewhere in the trees. He made a move to investigate and as he did so his foot caught on a section of broken rail and he went tumbling to the ground. His gun was jarred from his grasp and when he looked up it was to find the muzzle of a rifle pointed straight at his head. He raised his eyes to see the leer on the face of the unknown gunman as his finger tightened on the trigger. Events seemed to freeze and Brewer knew that his time was up.

A roaring silence filled his ears. He could only watch as the trigger was pulled back with what seemed infinite slowness, then everything speeded up again. To Brewer's amazement the rifle did not explode. Instead the man

215

suddenly dropped away from his field of vision. Then, in a deluge of noise and movement he heard a scream and the trampling of hoofs.

Brewer rolled to one side and saw the pinto, Flume, rearing up on its hind legs to bring its front hoofs crashing down on the gunman's chest. The man tried to scream once more but only a gurgled frothy moan emerged from his lips. The pinto reared one more time before Brewer called for it to stop. He got to his feet, ran to the horse and grasped it by its mane. The horse struggled, then began to calm down as Brewer talked to it.

'Steady, boy. OK, you done well. Good boy.'

The pinto grew less agitated although its ears remained pricked. Brewer stroked its nose. He didn't like to look down on the bloody mess of his would-be killer. After some moments he led the horse back into the woods, to protect it from any stray bullets.

'I guess you and me's even now,

Flume,' he whispered.

When he was satisfied that the horse had settled he looked back through the trees at the ranch house. The sounds of fighting had almost died away and it was clear that the struggle had been decided. The remaining attackers had taken to their horses and some of the hands who had been defending the ranch house were already trying to douse the fire in the barn, although it was a losing battle. Brewer made his way back to do what he could to help.

Curly Evans had taken charge of the operation but it was soon obvious to him that the best thing would be simply to abandon the barn and concentrate on preventing the flames from spreading to any of the other buildings. Curly rapped out his instructions; by nightfall the fire was out and the barn was a burnt-out smoking cinder. It didn't matter to Hethridge. It could be rebuilt. All he was concerned about was the fact that his daughter was safe.

The Lone Pine had survived the

worst that Sloane could throw at it and Hethridge had received confirmation earlier that day that there had been no further incidents with the cattle drive, which was well on its way to the rail head. The marshal had left, taking Choate along with him. If he had needed any further proof of Sloane's villainy, he had it in plenty now.

Late that night a small group of people were gathered on the veranda of the Lone Pine ranch house. Brewer and Josie were sitting together, hand in hand, while Hethridge, Drewitt and Riley drew on their cigars and enjoyed a bottle of the ranch owner's best brandy. After a time they were joined by Curly Evans.

'So we were right about Sloane,' Drewitt remarked. 'He was the real villain behind all this. What if he tries to get away?'

'He won't get far,' Hethridge replied. 'The marshal is takin' a trip to the Buzzard first thing tomorrow.'

'He probably thinks he's still got

Burke on his side,' Riley said. 'Reckon he's gonna be in for a big surprise.'

'Yeah,' Hethridge said. 'Guess I got the marshal all wrong after all.'

'The marshal's OK,' Riley said. 'All he needed was a little guidance.'

'And you were just the one to provide it,' Drewitt added.

Curly raised his eyes towards the river. 'The Deep Fork will be flowin' again soon,' he said.

Riley let out something between a growl and a laugh. 'Good thing in the end that they blocked it up,' he said. 'Otherwise I don't know if I'd have got that stagecoach across.'

Brewer looked over at him. 'That was some trip,' he said. 'Remind me never to ride shotgun with you again.' He laughed.

The others did so too.

'Hey, I wonder what happened to the dummy?'

They laughed again.

'I got kinda attached to that fella,' Riley said.

Josie looked up at Brewer and shivered. 'That dummy saved your life,' she whispered.

Brewer had said nothing about Flume and how the horse had saved him too. The pinto was safe in its stall with an extra supply of feed.

They lapsed into silence. The night was still and mild. From the trees behind the ranch house an owl hooted. Brewer squeezed Josie's hand and she looked up at him and smiled.

'You plannin' to carry on drivin' the stage?' Drewitt said, turning to Riley.

Riley's eyes shifted to the shattered wreckage lying in the blackened dirt of the ranch house yard.

'Guess it might be time to retire,' he replied.

* * *

Out on the prairie a campfire blazed. Everard Hite had decided it might be judicious to leave the town of Eagle Creek and the territory behind. In order to avoid possible complications he had left a letter for the marshal outlining everything he had learned about the suspicious circumstances surrounding Sloane's acquisition of the Buzzard On A Rail. This included details concerning the background of the former owner, who had made his pile working at the diggings. These details almost proved that he had meant to leave the Buzzard On A Rail, on his decease, to his former partner, a certain Rufus Riley. If the marshal was so minded, he could follow it up and add further charges to the ones already facing Sloane.

Hite sighed and felt lonely. It was good long ride to the nearest railroad stop. Maybe he should have waited for the stage. He drew his coat about him and moved closer to the fire.

He reached into an inside pocket and withdrew a sheaf of papers: the false documents he had been drawing up on Sloane's behalf. Sloane wouldn't need them now and they might be incriminating. He threw them on the fire.

He felt a little nervous. He was not used to riding alone like this and there was just a chance that Sloane might have set one of his hardcases on his trail. It hadn't been wise to try and get more money out of Sloane. Still, he had got enough out of the whole affair to be able to set himself up somewhere else. Yes, it could have turned out a lot worse. Now he would travel the railroad to somewhere new, somewhere fresh. Somewhere a long way from the Buzzard On A Rail.

It was long after midnight when silence descended at last on the Lone Pine. Everyone had turned in for the night except for Brewer and Josie who had wandered hand in hand to the banks of the Deep Fork. Slowly they strolled along the damp riverbed, passing the spot where the wheels of the coach had gouged out a section of the bank. The ruts they had made stretched away towards the ranch house, vanishing into the distance. Brewer raised his eyes. In an upper window one lamp dimly burned.

'That Riley can sure handle a stage,' Brewer remarked. 'I never figure to take a ride like that again.'

He paused and they were quiet for a moment.

'I owe him a lot,' he mused.

'We both owe him,' Josie replied.

She moved close to him and he held her, smelling the fragrance of her hair; neither of them spoke for a long time. Thoughts of the oldster soon vanished from their minds. They were together at last, something that seemed to them as strange and wonderful as the night where, just over their heads, the stars wheeled and blazed.

Back at the ranch house Whipcrack Riley leaned out of an upstairs window and surveyed the scene. He had watched Brewer and Josie as they set off for the river till they had merged into the night. He turned down the kerosene lamp.

'That old hoss Flume weren't the only critter to get caught in a quicksand,' he reflected. 'But he was the only one needed rescuin'.'

Other titles in the
Linford Western Library:

WHEN LIGHTNING STRIKES

Ethan Flagg

Lightning Cal Gentry's reputation as a lethal gunfighter has its downsides: he faces hotheads making their play, and hardcases who want respect and fame. It's hard to remain at the top — and now Cal wants out. But when he guns down Billy Vance in the New Mexico town of Tucumcari, it prompts a manhunt, putting his loved ones in mortal danger. Only with the help of the infamous renegade Apache, Geronimo, can he hope to resolve the issue.

SHOWDOWN IN JEOPARDY

John Davage

Near Cutler's Pass, a derailed train is raided for its $80,000 gold shipment . . . Five years later in the town of Jeopardy, Clyde Pascoe is shot and killed by an unknown assassin. Sheriff Cyrus Yapp and newspaper editor Will Bullard link Pascoe's death with the Cutler's Pass train raid. They suspect that a newcomer to Jeopardy, Luke Frey, is involved in the murders suddenly occurring in Jeopardy . . . whilst Luke's interest lies in discovering the identity of the train's mysterious fifth raider . . .